Sniffing Out Trouble

LAYERS OF MYSTERY
BOOK TWO

LEANNE BAKER

Sniffing Out Trouble
Paperback Edition
Copyright © 2022 CKN Christian Publishing

CKN Christian Publishing
An Imprint of Wolfpack Publishing
9850 S. Maryland Parkway, Suite A-5 #323
Las Vegas, Nevada 89183

cknchristianpublishing.com

Print ISBN 978-1-63977-115-8
eBook ISBN 978-1-63977-114-1
LCCN 2022948931

Sniffing Out Trouble

Chapter One

Trouble just opened the front door of Layers Bakery. He blew in with the sharp hint of an early fall Eastern Sierra breeze. Orange and red leaves swirled into the shop, bringing trouble with a capital *T* with them. My heart jumped against my ribcage as I searched his face for points of recognition. It had been long enough that I doubted my own eyes.

Was it him? My cousin Melody's brother?

Tall and lanky, six feet or more, shoulder-length dark ponytailed hair with threads of silver at the temples, bright blue eyes that always saw deep into my soul, where I used to believe no one else could. Tanned from working in the sun, bearing the same smile that used to charm the most frozen iced hearts. Yes, it's him. Mark, the Gibson black sheep.

"Sarah. Glad I found you."

The years and tears melted away. He was my cousin, the bad boy of Bishop as he was known in high school. Two years older than me and often in trouble. I'll never know how he graduated from high school. I always thought the teachers passed him to get him the heck out of town. And there was never any doubt he'd leave. They'd never admit it, but I suspected his parents were happy to see his dust.

"Mark?" My voice sounded shrill, even to my own ears. The kneading in the back room stopped, and I pictured the pair of bakers peering around the door. I struggled to collect my thoughts.

"The one and only." His broad smile accented both his hands that encompassed his wonderful self. He stood before me in a faded plaid long-sleeved sun shirt, jeans, and tennis shoes.

I snorted. Mark's distinct lack of humility had always put me off. Arrogant was his middle name. Darn him for rattling me so. Shame on me for letting it happen. I twisted around in time to see Marie and Charlie wide-eyed, watching from the kitchen. I flashed a tense smile, and they disappeared.

The reason Mark was in town wasn't a secret. In fact, the family should've anticipated his return. He'd always loved Melody. They were almost like twins except for the two-year age gap and angel and devil dispositions. How did he hear of her death?

"Did your mom tell you about Mel?" Anna, his mother. Of course. I remembered last month when we went through Melody's belongings. Melody's husband Wesley had handed Anna her phone and asked her to make any appropriate calls. She would've found his phone number on Melody's phone.

He tossed his head, flipping his long hair back in a familiar gesture. Mark looked around the bakery without answering. No doubt he'd sworn an oath not to tell who'd reached out to him. Not that he'd respect a promise. Too bad he couldn't have come in time for the funeral.

Or maybe it was better he'd missed it. "Do your folks know you're here?" With Tom and Anna on a horse drive for the rest of the week, I doubted it. They wouldn't have their cell phones with them. The lack of service on the trail made them unnecessary paperweights. The horse drive began in the summer corrals at a pack station in Mammoth Lakes, California, and ended close to our home in the Owens Valley in Bishop, California. With the exception of trailered-in horses for sleigh rides in Mammoth Lakes at Christmas, all stock had to be moved to a warmer area. The unpopulated areas between offered no amenities but especially no cell service. They had probably left the phones in their car.

"They're on a horse drive and won't be back until Saturday. Maybe you should've called first." I detested being snarky, but sometimes I couldn't help myself.

Mark's lips curled in a tiny snarl, and he turned away, leaning on the display case. "Sensible Sarah, always the one who follows the rules."

"That's me." I slammed the register. My nickname was wearing thin in these post-divorce days. More and more, it felt like 'sensible' was a synonym for 'dull.' "What are you planning to disrupt with your visit?" I didn't even try to keep the sarcasm out of my voice. I loved this man yet detested everything he stood for. His entire history had been about making others prove their love for him. And it was never enough for him. Yet, he was a protective cousin to an only child while growing up—me. My indebtedness masqueraded as affection for many years.

Mark slid around the counter to the opening. He faced me, his shoulders rigid, hands gripping in and out of fists, the only signs of his grief. "Tell me what happened to my sister, Sarah."

I sighed. He'd loved his sister. Not enough to stay and weather the storm of his making, but he loved her. "This isn't the place or the right time." As if to spare me further explanation, a middle-aged woman with two young children pushed open the front door and glided to the counter. "Do you have any crullers left?"

Mark leaned on the corner of the display, fading into the background during the transaction. He materialized when the shop bell announced they were gone.

"You're right." He pulled out a wooden coffee stirrer from the latte bar. "You're always right, Sarah. That's why people rely on you." He bent the stick until it broke, then broke it again.

"We close at two. I'll meet you at Mom and Dad's house."

"You don't get a coffee break?" He tilted his head like he was twelve again. Endearing, cajoling, getting his way. I marveled at the lightning-quick changes in his demeanor.

The bakery phone rang. I dodged Mark's question by answering the phone. "Layers Bakery."

"Sarah? Sarah, this is Javier at Boulangerie. I need your help."

"Sure." I'd known Javier, the Boulangerie Bakery manager, for a few months. We'd worked together and developed a friendship that transcended the threatening petty rivalries between competing bakeries. "What's going on?"

"He's at it again, Sarah." Javier's voice broke. "He's losing it this time."

"Losing what?" I knew he referenced his boss, the temperamental, micromanaging owner of Boulangerie,

Reginald Bateau. It's what he was losing that confused me.

"He's fired us all. We're clearing out, but I don't trust him. He's acting all crazy, throwing pans around. I'm afraid he might hurt himself." Javier huffed into the phone. "Please, Sarah. You're the only one he listens to."

That was up for debate, so I let the comment pass. "Have you called the police?"

"Not yet. You can help better than they can." Javier was breathing heavily into the phone.

"Has he hurt anyone?"

"Not so far." Pans clattered in the background. I recognized Reginald's voice, shouting and cussing. Voices in Spanish hurrying each other to get out.

I looked at the wall clock, eleven o'clock. I was tied to the front counter for another hour, at least. "I'll get there as soon as I can." Boulangerie was on the opposite side of Main Street, a half mile away from Layers. I'd have to drive.

Disconnecting, I snapped at Mark. "I can't talk now. Meet me at Mom's."

He slammed a hand on the counter. "Sarah, this is more important than…"

"No." My eyes held his in a vise. "It's not. Meet me later."

I turned away. Thinking fast, I ticked off my options. The fall interns hadn't yet been selected, and Emma, our barista, had left for greener pastures in Reno. Tiffani, her replacement, hadn't yet started. The head baker, Libby, was off today, so I called Charlie to the counter. Short and stocky, the baker's assistant reminded me of Popeye the Sailor—all muscles and mouth. Yet he was evolving into a skilled baker, picking up expertise from Libby in record speed. He'd never worked the cash register but now was as good a time as any. His co-worker, Marie, labored away in the back. She was so quiet; I'd taken to thinking of her as a mouse. The young college student, with delicate features and silent as a ghost, was elbow-deep in tomorrow's French bread, making Charlie the sole candidate to work the front.

At the door, Mark shouted, "I'm staying at Wesley's." I heard the tinkle of the bell, then the rattle of the door shaking shut. Mark was angry. I'd deal with him later. I thought about how my cousin Melody's husband felt about her brother staying at their house. Melody would have welcomed him, but Wesley had witnessed the damage Mark had done to the Gibson family. Even being a pastor, forgiving his brother-in-law would be difficult. And Melody wasn't there to greet him. Melody was dead.

In ten minutes, I had Charlie successfully tutored on the register. In the kitchen, Marie assured me she was set for the rest of today. I scratched out a checklist for tomorrow morning's set up—all the tasks she needed to prepare for Libby.

I took five minutes to gather my belongings. I had no idea how long this would take. I called for Rusty, my golden retriever/Irish setter mutt who napped in the upstairs office. When I reached for the back doorknob, I paused with a sigh.

I felt like I was going from one drama to the next.

Chapter Two

The sun and high desert heat blasted me when I opened the back door. The asphalt in the small four-space parking lot to the rear of the building would be too hot for Rusty's feet, so I squinted and rushed to my car. I opened the door for Rusty, and he hopped in. Starting up the car, I pushed on the air conditioner and waited for a minute until it blew cool air. He'd be fine for a few minutes. I closed the door.

Still blinded, I fished around my purse for sunglasses and slipped them on. A white van blocked my Camry in. Dented with rust spots on the fenders, I made a snap judgment. Either a skateboarder or a rock climber.

The shop on the corner, Owens Valley Sports, catered to the young skater clientele, so I chanced a guess. I marched across the street. I poked my head in the front door and shouted over the reggae music, "Olive, any of your customers have a white van? It's blocking me in."

Olive, the youthful shop employee, glanced around and repeated my question. "Anyone here drive a white van?"

A muffled voice came from a dressing room. "I'll be right there... get my pants on."

I blew out my tension, knowing I had to wait. Any urging from me wouldn't necessarily hurry up the process. I had to be patient.

Time had a different valuation here in my hometown of Bishop. But no matter how hard I watched the clock, I still waited for Mister Britches to come move his van. These five minutes were excruciating.

Reginald was physically trashing the Boulangerie Bakery. This was going on while I waited for some kid to move his illegally parked van. I could only hope Javier had gotten everyone out. I doubted his employees would call the police. How could the cops help? Reginald is the owner of the bakery, and destroying one's own property wasn't against the law. Besides, I doubted many of the mostly Hispanic employees trusted the police enough to call them for help.

And Mark's timing couldn't have been worse. I'd see him later at Mom and Dad's, then recalled he said he was staying with Wesley. I wondered if Wesley knew. I should call him while I waited. I tapped Wesley's call icon on my phone, and he picked up immediately. In the past few months since Melody's death, we'd grown closer, better friends than ever.

Rumbling from the dressing room distracted me. A suntanned young man with a head full of Rastafarian dreadlocks fell out of the room—thankfully with his pants on. He pulled his keys out of a pocket and, with an apologetic grin, strolled past me. Patchouli didn't mask his natural body smell.

Wesley answered. "Wesley. Did you know Mark is in town?"

"What? No." The one syllable faded out into a miserable tone that only Mark could evoke.

"He just showed up at Layers, but I got called away. He said he was staying with you."

Wesley's sigh confirmed what I suspected. Mark hadn't asked Wesley to stay at his sister's house. At the risk of being called a meddler, I felt I owed it to Wesley to warn him about Mark's arrival. So now, Wesley was alerted, and the purpose of my call was accomplished.

I watched the Rasta dude amble across the street and get into his van. A dark cloud of exhaust blew out as he started it up. Engine running on only a few of its cylinders, it sputtered onto the street, stalled, then lurched forward.

"Wesley, I've gotta go. We'll talk later." I disconnected and trotted to my Camry. Glancing at my phone, I figured twenty minutes had passed since Javier called.

I'd better hurry.

Chapter Three

Boulangerie was quiet when I drove into the empty parking lot. No one around. I'd prepared my "calm down" argument with a paraphrase from our high school political science teacher who'd taken it from the former governor of Virginia. "Anger doesn't solve anything. It builds nothing but can destroy everything." Reginald was two years ahead of me. Come to think of it, I wasn't sure that he took that class at all. But I did recall his wife Judith acting as a poli-sci teaching assistant in her last semester.

In the shade of a lush catalpa tree, I left the Camry with the air conditioning blasting for Rusty. A glance at the front door told me someone had the sense to turn the door sign to *Closed*. The handle was locked under my grip, as I'd expected. I walked around the French chateau-style building and found the back door sitting open. No noise.

When Javier had called, I'd heard the chaos Reginald had caused over the phone. But now, there was nothing going on at all. My neck hairs stood up. This wasn't right. I'd left my phone in the car—dumb, right? Deciding not to go back, retrieve it, and call 911, like a sensible person would, I used my toe to open the door all the way.

The kitchen was a shambles. Reginald had flung pots, pans, and pastries to the floor. The walls were covered with custard, blackberry and raspberry sauce, and pastry dough stuck to the shelves. Bread and rolls littered the floor. It would take days to clean this up and another couple to get the kitchen up and running again.

"Hello? Reginald?"

Silence.

"Reginald? Are you all right?" Dread oozed through me. The silence was frightening after what I'd heard on Javier's phone. Something was very wrong. As I turned, I caught sight of a foot behind a wheeled stainless baking rack.

I tiptoed between smashed cookies, rounded the corner, and caught my breath.

Reginald lay on the floor, a bread knife stuck out of his chest, one of two stab wounds in his upper torso. A pool of blood had seeped around each wound. I ran over to him, ignoring the food smashed into the cement floor. I reached down, my fingers searching for a pulse under his wrist. Nothing.

Nor was he breathing.

But he couldn't have breathed. What I saw was so incomprehensible that it didn't register for a moment. Reginald's mouth was open and filled with bright pink rosettes of icing, his eyes and nose packed with green star-shapes piped from a pastry bag. Both bags lay used and now innocuous, as if ready for the next dessert, on the worktable near Reginald's body.

My stomach roiled, threatening to return my breakfast. A gasp escaped, and I knew I had to get to my phone. I ran outside to my car.

"Bishop 911. What is your emergency?" A calm, masculine voice answered.

"I'm at Boulangerie Bakery on Main Street," I began, astonished at how my voice quivered. "Reginald... the owner. He's dead. Stabbed." I quit talking and let relief take over. Help was on the way.

"Is the person who stabbed him there?"

"No..." I hadn't looked around. The relief I'd felt fled in a hurry. The killer could still be in the building. It was a two-story shop, more than ample room to hide. "At least, I don't think so. I don't see anyone."

"Do you feel safe staying there? Or do you want to wait outside?"

"I'm outside right now. I don't know where I feel safe." I dropped to the driver's seat and sighed, keeping the phone line open as the dispatcher instructed. Rusty's head bobbed in excitement at my arrival. I opened the back door and let him out, keeping him in the shade while he watered the tree trunk. The day's temperatures still made the asphalt sizzle. I restricted him to the shade, then dropped to the back seat with the door open, my hand on Rusty's leash.

Chapter Four

I didn't hear sirens, so it was a surprise when a pair of patrol cars pulled up at the curb a few minutes later. Those two minutes seemed to take forever. An ambulance staged across the street, blocking traffic with its red rotating lights on.

The dispatcher disconnected with me as a gray-haired police officer scurried through the lot toward the back door, hunched over with his gun drawn. A blond female officer followed in the same stance, then made a quick turn to the front of the store.

"Has anyone left?" He kept his eyes on the building as he asked the question. The blond officer passed him and took a strategic position outside the back door.

"No."

"Stay here."

"Yes, sir." I had no intention of leaving. I knew what responsibility I had because of my career choice. As a former Los Angeles County court reporter who worked at downtown LA courthouses, I was familiar with police procedure. Most of my career, I'd worked recording criminal trials. I knew the police would search and clear the building, then contact me. I stayed put.

Rusty squirmed behind me into the back seat. He heard a rattling noise—it sounded like a pot fell inside. Then he sat alert and curious about the activity.

My attention fell to the reflection in the plate glass window opposite where I sat. I saw myself, with Rusty hovering. Even at this distance of fifteen feet, I saw the lines of strain in my oval face. I didn't look too bad for a woman in her mid-thirties, although I had seen better days. Brown shoulder-length hair in a pageboy style, more from negligence than styling. Active but not athletic, I thought my posture stated I looked beaten. I sat in an uncharacteristic hunch, waiting for the ugliness in the shop to end. Me being this rattled would not have been normal, but this was a shocking situation.

Four months before, I'd found the body of my dearest cousin, the victim of a murder. I thought about death and all that I'd been taught in Sunday school. The gift of life on earth and the promise of eternity. What about those loved ones left behind? I had zero to bequeath. Life was programmed for the parents to go before the children. I'd be alone after Mom and Dad died. I had no husband or children. No legacy. No one to give anything to. I thought of Melody and the finality of her death. What are the chances similar circumstances could be repeated? My stomach churned as visions of Cousin Melody's body played in my head.

Now to be joined by my nemesis, Reginald Bateau.

I stood to distract myself from stewing in foul memories. Making a conscious decision to be mindful of my surrounding, I watched the activity around me. In the days before I left town, Bishop PD rarely had more than two sworn officers on at any time during the day. Given the fiscal constraints of the day, I doubted the department had grown. Any major incident within the city limits would've required assistance from outside agencies. My glimpse took in the Inyo County sheriff, the California Highway Patrol directing traffic around the emergency vehicles parked on Main Street, and a Fish and Game warden.

This was more than mutual aid. These men and women depended on each other for backup when needed. Inyo law enforcement officers knew they should respond to another agency as needed so that when assistance was necessary, they would get it in return. It was a symbiotic relationship between local, state, and federal organizations that worked well for this isolated area.

A Bishop officer, this one a sergeant from the stripes on his sleeve, approached me. Salt-and-pepper hair and a physique grown chunky with age, he gave me an awkward smile. Trying to flatten a stubborn cowlick in a nervous gesture, he asked. "Miss, did you see anyone around the building or lot when you arrived?"

"No."

"You're the caller?"

"Yes."

"So, you're the last person to see the victim."

I shrugged. "I saw him deceased. The last person to see him would be the killer."

"Why did you come here today?" His lips thinned as he fished out a notebook and pen from his breast pocket.

"I got a call from Javier, the manager. He told me Reginald was losing it. He wanted me to come help because Reginald seemed to listen to me—sometimes."

"What's Javier's last name?" The sergeant's name tag read, *Foster*.

"Uran."

He scribbled in his notebook.

He straightened and studied me. "Your name? Address?"

I'd been around the court long enough to know not to volunteer anything during an interview. I kept my answers short. "Sarah Murray. 1399 McLaren Lane."

"What's your occupation?" Apparently, he'd not found me interesting enough to study. He focused on his notebook.

"I manage Layers Bakery at the moment."

A glance in my direction. "What do you mean, 'at the moment'?"

I made it as simple as I could. "The bakery is temporary. I'm a court reporter, and I've got the promise of a job working for Inyo County sometime after the new year."

He lasered in on me again. "And how did you know the victim?"

I sighed, glad I'd organized my thoughts while waiting for the cops to finish in the building. "I helped Reginald out when his business was in trouble four months ago. All his employees walked out on him. He brokered a deal with them to come back if I came in and managed the place. I did that. After a few weeks, he didn't appreciate that the bakery was more profitable than it had been under his management. By mutual agreement, I left. I also suggested Javier replace me."

Sergeant Foster nodded, his blue eyes giving away that he believed there was more to my story.

As much as it pained me, I decided to be more forthcoming. "You'll know that the victim was on supervised recognizance for assault. The victim was my cousin,

Melody Charters, who was subsequently murdered by Grant Armstrong. I also found her body."

He gave a final nod and turned away to speak into his shoulder mic. I thought I heard "animal control."

Foster flipped his notebook closed. Tucking it into his breast pocket, he said, "Miss Murray, come down to the station, and we'll take a formal statement from you. There's clearly more information we need you to give us." He motioned to a patrol car parked on Main Street.

I half expected to get handcuffs slapped on my wrists. "What are you doing? Arresting me?" I knew this wasn't a formal arrest, but I didn't like this guy flexing his legal muscle at me. "A detention?"

"No, Miss Murray. This isn't a detention. You are free to go at any time."

I took a step closer to him. "Okay. If that's the case, cancel animal control. The dog stays with me. I'll drive to the station in my own car."

His eyes narrowed, and he huffed his miscalculation. He couldn't counter this unless he arrested me—for which he had no cause.

"I'll follow you." He turned and spoke into his mic again.

Chapter Five

"You understand that I'm looking at you for this homicide, Miss Murray."

"Then you're wasting your time." I'd never had a temper, but Sergeant Foster brought a bright, shiny anger out in me. And I was irritated at being called *miss*. "There's a murderer out there who you're ignoring."

The sergeant's chin turned to granite. "Don't tell me how to do police work."

Arguing with him was like talking to a wall—I'd get nowhere fast.

Earlier, he'd ticked off the points to make his argument. "One, you have a motive: He's the guy who incapacitated your cousin, enabling another to finish her off. Two, you have opportunity: we only have your word for your alibi timeline. How long would his murder have taken? Two seconds for the stabbing, five for the 'decorations.'" He crooked his finger around the last word for emphasis. "And you work at a bakery, so you'd know how to work one of those pastry bags."

"You're reading too much into this. Anyone could do

the decorations. It's not rocket science." I thought he tended toward drama more than facts. And the fact was, I hadn't killed Reginald Bateau, no matter how many fingers the sergeant ticked off. I looked over my statement one last time and signed it. "I stand by this statement." Shoving it across the desk, I asked, "Now can I go?"

Foster glanced at the clock on the wall and stood. I was being dismissed. Rusty had been lying in a corner and rose with me. Foster walked me out to the lobby and looped his arms across his chest at the front door.

I didn't say goodbye. Nor did he.

Finally, in the Camry with Rusty breathing down my neck, I let the car's air conditioning blast me in the face. I was drenched with perspiration. I'd only been outside for a few minutes, so I decided that Sergeant Foster had made me sweat. While he was merely doing his job, I believed he played the heavy too easily. In truth, I didn't think he did his job very well. There were plenty of other people in town with a stronger motive than mine. Reginald might have been local business royalty, but he wasn't well-liked. Besides, I hadn't held Reginald's actions against him. He was on the road to Inyo County justice—a road I had no desire to travel. While justice was in my wheelhouse, vengeance was not.

I stopped by Layers to check on Charlie. He was enjoying this change in his routine and was happy to finish out the day at the counter. It would only be for another hour anyway. Libby had come in to check on Marie and was in the back, cleaning up. She looked so serious that I didn't want to disturb her.

Clipped on the whiteboard I'd installed next to the kitchen landline, I found a note addressed to me. Charlie had scrawled, *call Paula at the chamber of commerce*. I could barely read the phone number and decided I'd call her tomorrow. I didn't feel like talking to a stranger today.

I didn't want to be alone. I punched the icon for Jake's phone number, then disconnected. What could my boyfriend do? He was a seven hours drive away. Even as a police lieutenant for the Northern California town of Petaluma, he had no jurisdiction here. I also knew that cops were loath to exercise their authority across area boundaries. I'd wait to tell him. He'd be here this weekend anyway. It would be better face-to-face. He wouldn't have to worry about me between now and then, at least.

Libby? No. My head baker was turning into a dear friend, but she was eighteen. While she was mature beyond her years, she had her own demons to wrestle. Her father had been arrested for Melody's murder two months ago. Melody had mentored Libby at the bakery, at school, and beyond. To find out her father killed her mentor almost shattered her. From what I saw today, she was preoccupied with something serious. I didn't want to disturb her. It was enough for her to show up and bake at four-thirty in the morning six days a week.

All my high school girlfriends had left town, most of them married with their own families. I'd lost touch with the majority and felt awkward about calling anyone still here after I'd been back in Bishop four months and had neglected to contact any of them.

Mom and Dad had left for their semiannual horse drive and were on the trail with Anna and Tom. They weren't due back for six more days.

Wesley. He would understand. Especially him. He'd been arrested for Melody's murder early on by the Inyo County sheriff, looking for an easy notch for his tough-on-crime campaign promises. Thankfully, Wesley's father hired a sharp attorney who poked giant holes in the sheriff's case. Subsequently released without charge, Wesley was busy recovering from the loss of his wife and trying to rebuild his scandalized church flock.

Busy or not, I knew he'd be there for his wife's cousin—me.

Chapter Six

Wesley drove into the U-shaped driveway of my parents' McLaren area home right after I parked. I'd let Rusty out to pee and stood waiting on the concrete. Wesley must have been in town, maybe at the New Life Fellowship, his church on the North Sierra Highway. Had he been at home in Wilkerson, it would've taken twenty minutes to get to what was my temporary home. Wesley's aging and sun-bleached RAV4 screeched to a halt behind me. He flung the door open, leaving the car running. He sprinted to me and grabbed my arms. Rusty ran to him but was ignored.

"Are you all right?" His dark blond curls shook as he looked me over head to toe. He had a pleasant face, a great attribute for a pastor.

I nodded, then allowed myself to crumple into his arms. He understood my situation. Tears came but passed quickly as anger pushed them aside. I pulled away, and he handed me a tissue. "Let's go inside. It'll be cooler."

My parents' home was a large ranch-style on the edge

of Bishop. It was mid-century vintage but had been maintained and updated. The air conditioning worked like a dream.

Home was Bishop, California, a rural high desert town with a population of 3,700 nestled in the Owens Valley and 4,151 feet above sea level. The surrounding Great Basin terrain is bordered by the Sierra Nevada Mountain range to the west and the White Mountains to the east. The nearby ranching and farming communities accounted for another fourteen thousand residents. Tourism kept the financial lifeblood pumping. Fishing, hiking, and camping in the summer, then winter sports, including skiing and snowboarding at nearby Mammoth Mountain Ski Area, a mere forty-three miles north and 3,729 feet higher at 7,880 feet. The Paiute Shoshone Reservation bordered the city limits to the west occupying a large rural area.

Bishop was a huge change from the past ten years I spent in Los Angeles. An ugly divorce had brought me home, and after four months, I was settling in and learning to be a single person. Mom and Dad let me bunk with them until I got my feet back under me. I had the promise of a county job as a court reporter, in January, which would enable me to be self-sufficient. Beyond that, I hadn't done much planning for my future. My own home, sure. Marriage, doubtful. I'd made a mess of my romantic relationships so far and wasn't all that eager to commit, even though I was interested in Jake.

For now, I managed my cousin Melody's bakery and culinary education nonprofit. She'd been killed in May, leaving the family and the Bishop community reeling. The murderer was connected to Melody's direct competition, Boulangerie Bakery, and its owner Reginald Bateau.

Melody's dream had been to open a bakery. Layers

Bakery was open a mere six months before it started showing a solid profit. Soon, the bakery went beyond earning money. Melody had taken in an apprentice from the local continuation school, Libby Armstrong. Libby was also a neighbor. In the few months together, Melody bolstered Libby's ability to trust and gave her the confidence to begin to master baking pastries. Libby was now the Layers' head baker. She and I were working on helping other students in a similar predicament to build their culinary and service skills with an eye on future employment.

Wesley was an excellent listener and Melody's heir and actual owner of Layers. Besides being a pastor, he had a patient nature. I tried not to take advantage of him. He was a busy guy. But he knew about families and human nature. Wesley's father had been previously married. Their son Jake was born in 1984 in Petaluma, the north bay area of San Francisco. They divorced shortly after, and their father married his second wife from Palmdale. Wesley was born in 1985. Shortly after the family bought a vacation home in Starlite Estates outside of Bishop. Wesley's father was an extremely successful tax attorney and notoriously difficult to get along with. When Wesley's mother divorced him, she got the Starlite house, so mother and son stayed in Bishop. Wesley went to the same schools as Melody and me, but we weren't close until the junior year in high school.

With ice water all around, Rusty sat under my feet at the kitchen table as I explained to Wesley what happened at Boulangerie.

"We need to tell Jake. See what he says..." Wesley and Jake were brothers—half brothers, to be accurate. After being estranged because of divorces, they'd reconnected and had become close after the death of Jake's wife four years ago. Now, after Melody's death, they were almost inseparable. Except Jake lived 350 miles away.

I held up my hand to stop him. "No. I want to tell him in person. Otherwise, he'll worry, and I don't want that."

"Sarah." Wesley's voice was low. I've known him long enough to realize he's going to tell me what he thinks I need to hear, not what I'd *like* to hear. I can be stubborn and opinionated, but when I realize someone who cares about me is trying to steer me in a different direction for my own good, I listen. "Think about it. How would you feel if the situation was reversed? Wouldn't you be hurt at being excluded, even temporarily?"

I chewed my lip and thought it over. Jake couldn't do anything if he was here anyway. Maybe Wesley was right; honesty would go further than sparing his feelings for a few days. Besides, putting Wesley in the middle of a lie—even if it was merely an omission—was wrong. Wesley had his own struggles. He still mourned his wife. Without her income, I knew money was tight, even with the profits from Layers coming his way. He didn't need grief from me. I'd follow his suggestion.

"Okay. How about a FaceTime?"

Wesley nodded, picking up his phone. He punched in a text and waited. "I want to be sure he's available and not in a meeting or busy elsewhere."

A ding signaled his answer. This went on back and forth for a minute until Wesley sat next to me and propped up his phone.

I started to perspire again as the connection completed. This was going to be difficult, but my cousin was right, I had to be honest with Jake. He deserved that.

Wesley took over the call. "We're here at Sarah's folks' house. Something happened today that you should know about, not for what you can fix but what you can offer in the way of comfort."

Jake's puzzled face darkened at Wesley's words. He studied his brother's face, then mine.

There was no mercy in putting this off. "I got questioned about a homicide today."

Jake's face was the picture of control. No flaming out as my ex would've done, no anger or hostility. "Go on."

The words spilled out, even a few tears, but in the end, I was grateful for Jake's understanding.

"You're right, Wesley. I can't fix this. But as I see it, nothing's broken. You've got a hayseed cop who's looking at you for a crime you didn't commit. You were convenient. You weren't under arrest or even detained, so he doesn't have enough to charge you."

"I found the body…"

"…and he mistook your proximity and made you a person of interest." Jake finished my sentence and went on. "You're not a suspect. Unless some new evidence comes to light, you shouldn't be charged."

I breathed a bit easier, both at his thoughts and the delivery. He wasn't angry. He was thoughtful, considering all I'd told him. My heart moved another notch toward him. Ghosts from ten years of a temperamental, moody, and deceitful man had left scars. Enough damage that I was reluctant to consider a serious relationship.

Then I got to know Jake.

"One last thing," he said before he signed off. "I'd like to talk to Kelly about this. Is it okay with you, Sarah?"

Kelly McSorley was a deputy and trusted friend. We'd gone to high school together, and he'd proven himself to both Jake and me during the investigation of Melody's murder. "Yes, it's okay with me."

Heck, Kelly might even come up with something that could point to the real killer, given his professional association with Bishop PD.

Chapter Seven

After a goodbye to Jake, Wesley sat back in the kitchen chair. He stretched his legs out and tapped his chin thoughtfully. "I think the sergeant was jumping the gun to finger you as a suspect."

I nodded. If there was a strategy, it wasn't apparent to me.

He leaned in, meeting my gaze. "Do you think you need to hire an attorney? The guy my dad hired was good..."

"I'll wait until they have more evidence. I'll know if there are any imminent charges coming my way. If there isn't, I won't worry. Like your brother said, Foster doesn't have enough to charge."

He sat back and sipped his melted ice water. "It's crazy, don't you think?"

There was a lot crazy around here. I wasn't sure what he meant specifically.

At my blank look, he explained. "Reginald gets killed in the middle of town in the middle of the day." He shrugged. "No one was around. No one saw anything."

Now I got it. "Yes, it is crazy. How could this happen at eleven-thirty, the middle of the day? I mean, it must've taken a mere few minutes. I was on my way from Layers, driving up Main Street, when someone stabbed him and left those macabre decorations."

"At eleven-thirty?" Wesley's jaw dropped with amazement. "I was a few blocks away at the bank."

We sat in silence for a few moments. Something was bothering me. "What do you suppose the icing rosettes were about? Is there a message in there that I'm not getting?"

"Message?" He squinted with doubt. "You mean like a clue?"

"Clue?" I had to think about that. "No, I wouldn't necessarily know what to do with a clue. I'm not a cop, remember?"

He sat up and gave me a wry smile. "Right. You recall how instrumental you were in identifying Melody's killer, don't you?"

Perhaps I had meddled a bit there. "The cops got him, not me."

"You facilitated the whole plan to trap him. You put it together. If it hadn't been for you, Grant Armstrong would've gotten away with two murders."

I leaned back in my chair, rolling the sweating glass over my forehead. Air conditioning or not, I was warm. Wesley had a point. I was good at finding out people's secrets. I was a good listener and most, especially Bishop folk, were more inclined to speak to another Bishop girl than a Bishop cop. Besides, I couldn't sit around and wait to be arrested. I must actively search for the truth.

But I needed a plan. I'd figure something out later when I was alone.

For now, Wesley's family drama continued. "Mark Gibson was in the bakery this morning."

Wesley sighed. "I half expected him before this. Mel had kept in touch with him."

I must've looked surprised because he rushed to add, "On the Q.T., of course. Tom and Anna had no idea. Mel felt it was best that way." Melody would have wanted to spare their parents the pain of Mark's life.

The incident that had sustained the rift between son and parents was beyond me. I knew what happened, but couldn't understand how none of them made peace with each other. It had stretched on for years. No one spoke about it other than Tom, who said once that Mark was dead to him. It didn't surprise me that Melody would've kept in touch with her brother. It had been the two of them growing up together—and me. I *was* a little hurt that Melody hadn't told me. We had been close, we three. The last I'd heard, Mark was in Mexico, growing marijuana. But that was over ten years ago, before I married Blaine.

"Mark told me that he was staying with you."

Wesley lifted an eyebrow. "I guess he is. He's hardly welcome at Tom's. And I'm sure he couldn't afford a motel."

"They're gone anyway until Saturday." I shook my head in amazement at the turmoil Mark's arrival would cause. How would it be during his visit? Maybe Wesley could convince him to leave before the Gibsons returned from the drive. Yeah, and maybe it would rain money.

Mark was in Bishop for a purpose. That purpose defied my imagination. If he wanted to rub salt into his parents' grieving hearts, he would do it. If he wanted to make peace with them, return to the family, that was something else. Whatever his motive, I wanted no part of the impending spectacle.

I glanced at my phone. Where was Mark? He was supposed to meet me here.

Mark never showed that night. Nor was there a phone call. I had other worries to fret about, so I never gave Mark Gibson's absence another thought.

Chapter Eight

At Layers, midmorning the next day, I returned the call to Paula at the chamber. She greeted me warmly and asked if she could drop by as she was in the area. I agreed. The breakfast rush was over, and Charlie could handle the stragglers who walked in.

"I'm sorry we have to meet upstairs in the office. I have plans to include a café setup out front, but they're only plans at the moment."

A petite blond, Paula waved the apology away. "No worries. I'm here to see you wherever I can get you to sit still." I wondered at her statement. I'd heard from the chamber and the visitors' center shortly after my arrival. I'd squeezed out enough money from our tight budget to advertise in their newsletter. Paula passed on my offer of coffee and a pastry, and we marched upstairs to be greeted by my never-knew-a-stranger canine buddy, Rusty. With a swinging tail that could clear a coffee table, he sniffed her hand, looking for a dog treat. Thankfully, Paula was a dog person and petted Rusty. He appreciated the attention but preferred treats, so he walked back to his bed, twirled three times, and plopped back down to resume his nap.

"I'm sure you're curious about why I'm here, so I'll get right to the point. The chamber is organizing a new festival, and your name was presented as a person who could be in charge."

"Festival? I've never done anything like this before."

"The lack of experience isn't of concern. Everyone on the board agreed you'd be the perfect person to draw people together to get this done."

"I don't even know anyone on the board."

"You do. You just don't *know* you do." Her sweet smile made me feel like I was someone special—and the board knew it. I knew a con when I saw one.

"I'm sorry, but I don't..."

"Before you refuse, let me give you an idea of what this is about." She paused long enough for me to give in. "This area is prime territory for a Fall Colors event."

"Fall colors? Why that's only a month, maybe six weeks away."

"True, but I... we believe we can whip this up into a real event. Our goal is twofold. We want to raise money for the I Care for Pets of the Eastern Sierra nonprofit. The second goal is more self-serving. We want more visitors to the area and more customers in our stores."

I let her speak, recalling how I'd heard about the Stitch fund set up to assist shelter pets to get the veterinary care they needed. Dad told me about it after I found an injured stray. I'd taken the dog to the vet, willing to pay out of my own pocket. Thankfully, his owner had been found quickly. I was also thankful his owner turned out to be Jake Charters.

When I didn't protest, Paula took this as an opening. "What we envision is an event like this: a festival in City

Park, with an emphasis on outdoor activities. There is so much opportunity here for hiking and biking, fishing, camping, rock climbing, and a plethora of extreme sports." Did she really say *plethora*? "Aside from the US Forest Service and Bureau of Land Management, there are our local government organizations that could participate, like Inyo County search and rescue. Each has something to offer visitors. We'd also invite local vendors to assist visitors in making their dreams come true. For instance, if you're a rock climber, you could visit the Owens Valley Sports booth. If you're a fisherman, there's Mack's and Culvers, both of whom would love to participate."

I began to feel her excitement. "We could get hotels and restaurants to set up tables to book vacations. As well as all kinds of amenities for their visit to Bishop." One of the aspects I loved about this small town was the fact that it wasn't crowded, like LA. But make no mistake, it could support thousands more people, even at one time. Mule Days over Memorial Day weekend was proof after hosting over thirty thousand people annually. "The biggest hurdle will be the time frame. When are you planning on holding this festival?"

She squinted with doubt. It would be tight, for sure. "September twenty-fourth. It's the last Saturday of the month, and the trees in the Owens Valley should be in full colors by then. The higher elevations begin first, so folks coming from the Bay Area will have a real treat coming down 395."

I shook my head. Five weeks. That wasn't much time, but with help, it was doable. "How much help can I count on from the chamber?"

"We're one hundred percent committed. Ask anyone for anything, and we'll get it done."

"Has this been done before?"

Paula shook her head. "This will be the first. If all goes as well as we hope, we'll plan for next year."

I stretched out my hand, and she took it in a mighty grip. "Welcome aboard. I'll be your liaison. We have several volunteers from the board already. If I can help, holler."

"Sure. Just one more thing." I had to know. "Who recommended me?"

Paula displayed a coy smile. "I guess it's no secret. Frank Scherwin." At my quizzical look, she went on, "He's not actually on the board yet but will be when he retires. Besides being the police chief, he owns a photography business."

"I'm glad I could inspire such trust in my abilities." I said as I wondered what the heck I'd gotten myself into.

Chapter Nine

Shortly after Paula left, Libby ran out of the food coloring she needed for a special order. The new principal of Bishop High School ordered a 'welcome back' full sheet cake with the reds, oranges, and yellows of a fall colors design. Libby insisted she had to have MasterChef sunset orange and sky blue. That meant a trip to the restaurant supply store on the north end of town.

I left Rusty in the office as the day was warming already. We normally ordered online and had supplies delivered a few times in the past four months, but I'd had to trek northward to the store. While I knew where the Owens Valley Restaurant Supply was, I usually needed help navigating the aisles.

Today was no different. The store rarely boasted crowds, so it was easy to find an employee who would point me in the correct direction. A gaunt young man with stringy hair and a bad posture made me hesitate over my store choice. A glance at the floor told me the place was clean enough. And it was too late to go to a grocery and get retail food coloring. Besides, Libby didn't care for the volume that retail coloring bottles took to get her desired effect. I asked the employee for directions and got a nod over his shoulder. Just past the cleaning supplies, I saw a sign that read *Baking Supplies*, so at least I was in the right neighborhood.

I wended my way down an aisle filled with industrial cleaning materials. Halfway down, a woman carrying a plastic bucket bumped into me. "Oh, I'm sorry." was my automatic response. I turned to face her.

Carrot-orange hair upswept into an almost clichéd bouffant style startled me enough that I stared. At her sputtering, I finally looked at her face. Puffy and blotchy from too much alcohol and painted with makeup and a shade of lipstick that fought with her hair color, she was unmistakable.

Judith Bateau. I hadn't seen her since my high school years. She'd been ahead of me with Reginald. She'd been attractive then but hadn't so much as changed her hairstyle from thirteen years ago. These days she'd added a rayon scarf, gaudy necklaces, and arm bangles. It helped that I'd seen her picture on the wall at Boulangerie.

I held my breath. Seconds ticked by. How would she react to me?

She must have been as startled to see me. It didn't take long for her to regroup and go on the offensive—and I mean offensive. Her mouth twisted with revulsion. "You twit. What are you doing here? You should be in jail."

A teenage boy stamped with Reginald's features swept up beside her. "Is this the one who killed dad?" His arms were filled with jugs of industrial cleaners. I doubted they'd be allowed into Boulangerie today, but who knew with Sergeant Foster at the helm?

"Now, wait a minute. The police took my statement. That's all." No way I was going to pass on Sergeant Foster's suspicions.

"We heard you did it, but they don't have enough evidence to arrest you." Judith nodded at her son, who disappeared around the corner. The scrawny clerk peered at us over some boxes in the next aisle.

"Please, I know you're in shock and grieving. But I'm doing what I can to be honest with the police. I want to find the killer too."

Something in my tone must have reached Judith. Her spine relaxed, and her face softened. Tears pooled in her eyes, and I found myself reaching to her hand for comfort. "I'm so sorry for the loss of your husband, Judith."

She sniffled, and I handed her a tissue.

"Thank you. I'm sorry for what I said. There's just so much pressure now. I've got everyone in my family telling me what to do."

I gave her what I hoped was a sympathetic smile. "And losing Reginald is such a loss." I didn't want to entertain ideas on what a loss he was. He'd been a pain in my side since I returned to Bishop. Still, I hadn't wanted to calm his troublesome character in this manner.

"You have no idea." she sniffled into the wadded-up tissue.

I did, but she didn't need to know what I suspected. I squeezed her hand slightly. I looked over her shoulder at the *Baking Supplies* sign and took my hand back. I hoped this scene was over for now.

"He was a bully and a tyrant." she whispered.

"What?" Tell me something I don't know, I thought. I couldn't believe I'd heard it from his wife.

She eyed me like I was stupid and repeated, "he was a bully and a tyrant. You know I had to account for every cent I spent? He wouldn't let me buy new clothes." She smoothed her blouse. "This is twelve years old. Can you believe it? Why, right before he was killed, he called to harangue me about spending money. He kept telling me not to spend so much. But I didn't." She looked at me through watery, bloodshot eyes. I wondered if her tears were for his death or what she perceived would be her loss.

Her son returned, his arms laden with even more boxes of cleaners, wipes, and sponges. He stood beside his mother, his chin set in a belligerent underbite.

"Oh my." What could I say to that? She stood in the middle of a store, bad-mouthing her recently murdered husband. Even if he was all those things... It would give her motive. It wouldn't be the first time a wife had killed her husband. Looking at Judith in this new light made me wary.

"And my hair. My mother had to do my hair..." Her son shifted his load and tapped her on the shoulder, interrupting her tirade. She glanced at him as Ed Strange marched up the aisle. His long-sleeved button-up sun shirt, jeans, and tennis shoes only accented his almost comic Ichabod Crane posture. His shoulder-length hair was pulled back into a ponytail. He pushed up the nose-piece of his John Lennon-style glasses.

Ed's face darkened at the sight of me. He must have recalled our last meeting when he tried to intimidate me at Reginald's behest. He'd impersonated a building inspector who found multiple infractions in the Layers building. The implication was that he'd shut the bakery down. I'd called his bluff and humiliated him.

"You've got some nerve, bothering a grieving widow."

He put a protective arm around his sister. "Go away." With his other hand, he brushed me away like I was an annoying mosquito.

Dismissed in this way grated on my pride, but it was the means of an exit. I nodded respectfully at Judith and her son and brushed past Ed without a thought.

Chapter Ten

I sat in the car in the parking lot after buying the food coloring. While I waited for the air conditioning to cool the inside, I reviewed my encounter with Judith. Clearly, she wasn't too broken up about his demise—by whatever means. Although she may have had some feelings for him, she held onto her resentment and anger. It almost sounded like he was more controlling at home than at Boulangerie. It might have been a motive, but I couldn't reconcile the irate yet almost ditzy woman with the calculating vindictiveness of a killer who would deface a corpse like Reginald's was.

Until her death a few months ago, Reginald's mother ruled Boulangerie like the queen she thought she was. Her husband, Reginald the first, had started the bakery when he arrived in the Owens Valley after immigrating from France. He'd built an empire before his untimely passing two decades after starting the business. Reginald was old enough to take over the management under the strict guidance of his mother. The freedom he should have felt at her death wasn't constructive because he'd begun the same regimen of micromanaging that his mother had.

I didn't know what this chance conversation meant, but I was sure there was something at work. I just didn't know what.

The air finally cooled the interior as I concluded my thoughts. Since I was on the north end of town, I might as well stop into the feedstore and buy Rusty some kibble. Wye Road Feeds was less than a block away. I put the manager on my mental list of who to talk to about the Fall Colors Festival. But I had to get my plan together first.

I loved the inside of a feedstore. It was one of the many things I missed when I moved to LA. Whiffs of alfalfa and grass hay wafted through the huge roll-up door that led to the yard. Orderly rows of pet food—dog, cat, hamster, bird, and more defined the aisles. A rooster crowed in the distance. Two women at the counter debated different styles of horse halters. This place held fine memories—early spring shopping for chicks to supply eggs for mom's baking. Dad bought my first saddle here when I was eight. That had made me feel like I was a productive part of the family. After that, Dad made sure I helped Uncle Tom and Aunt Anna out in the spring and fall drives. Feedstores are some of the fondest memories of my childhood.

A familiar laugh punctured my remembrances. A loud, earthy hoot full of life. Emily?

I rounded the aisle and walked to the front counter. The two women were in deep debate over the merits of nylon versus jute halters and rope. The clerk behind the counter was suntanned in the way of a person who'd spent many hours in the saddle. "We don't carry anything but the nylon or polyester halters."

"Yeah, but these aren't authentic western materials."

Emily Kilbride looped her arms across her chest and let out a bellow again. "You're kidding, right?" Her curly red hair shook in disbelief as she beheld the fool in front of her.

"Well, no…"

Emily leaned across the counter. "Here's the deal. We're the only game in town for horse supplies. If you want something like jute, you're going to have to go online or to a specialty store." She straightened, eyeing this poor soul with the laser precision of a target finder. In Emily's words, she was saying, "Buy this or leave."

The woman huffed and turned away, making for the door. As she left, Emily finally saw past her. She shouted, "Sarah!" then rounded the counter and trotted toward me. I was soon returning her embrace. Em was a friend from high school, a stalwart companion during my extra-curricular yearbook work and Spanish Team adventures.

"I heard you were back in town." She held me at arm's length, looking me over. "Aw, honey. Sorry about the divorce. It doesn't look good on you."

Falling right in line with her usual brutal honesty, I took no offense. After all, I'd just been called out as a murderer in public, hadn't I?

But I was safe now. Emily had my back, no matter what. "It's been a bit rough since I got back."

Em looped her arm around mine and steered us to the counter. She waved at a stool, and I dropped onto it. Her face softened with compassion. "I heard about Mel. I'm so sorry."

I blew out a breath, the tension leaving me. "It was as bad as you'd imagine."

"I missed the memorial. The baby came down with a bad cold."

"Baby?" I'd missed so much in the ten isolated years I was married to Blaine. How I could've lost touch with such a dear friend mystified me. I know it wasn't all his fault but seeing Emily rekindled the warm feeling of being home. Emily's arms settled on her hips akimbo in a "tell me what's been happening" stance.

The door chime tinkled, and a pair of customers ambled in. "All right." She waved the thought away. "Later when we have more time."

Emily listened to the couple and pointed them in the direction of horse wormers. She grabbed my arm and poked her freckled face inches away from mine. "I've gotta ask you—what about this nonprofit you set up at the bakery?"

I shrugged. Where to start? "What have you heard?"

Emily rang up the wormers for the customers, handed them the receipt, and turned back to me. "My nephew, Julie's boy, is kind of borderline in school. He heard about this chef thing—"

"Baking," I corrected her. "It's called Better Off Baking."

"Okay, baking thing and wants to do it."

"We should meet for coffee, and I can tell you about it after you fill me in on the family. Did you marry Matt?"

Her broad smile admitted the crime. "Yep, and have four kids now. Best thing I ever did." Four kids? How could I have wasted so much time without starting a family? Blaine hadn't stayed in one place long enough to begin having kids. I never thought he wanted them. Besides, he was more a child than an adult. But me? I didn't feel the same way. Did that mean I wanted children?

I found myself a tad envious of my friend Emily. We set a date for the next day. I left with a forty-pound bag of dog food and a smile on my face.

I loved being home.

Chapter Eleven

"It took you long enough." Libby grabbed the food coloring and hunkered over her icing bowl. A slight eighteen-year-old wearing cargo shorts and a tank top under her apron. Her purple hair was cut short on one side and left long on the other. The nose ring and ear tunnel jewelry had made me wary when I first met her. But I trusted my cousin Melody's judgment. If she mentored Libby, she saw something special in her.

Special indeed. This young woman had blossomed under Melody's tutelage as a baker and a human being. This mentorship was the grain of sand that became the pearl of what is now Better Off Baking, or BOB for short.

"I got waylaid by the widow accusing me of her husband's murder."

Libby glanced up, her face twisted with disgust. "She's a piece of work, for sure." She tossed her long hair out of her eyes and pursed her lips. "I hope you didn't give her any respect."

Libby had her own problems to deal with, so I spared

her the details. "I saw her son. He should be about your age. Do you know him?"

"Devon?" She used a dropper to add green to the white icing in a small bowl. Another dropper for the orange in the next bowl. "Yeah, but he's a year behind me at Bishop High. Smart kid but kind of a goof. Not real good with people. He used to get pushed around a lot." She whisked the green icing until it was blended. Then the same with the orange. "His father was the west coast distributor of bullying."

She paused and squinted. "Yeah, I remember seeing the dad drop Devon off at school one day. I heard the old man yelling half a mile away. I felt sorry for Devon." She shrugged; this objectionable behavior was a part of life in which she didn't want to dwell. Her own father had done much worse. He'd killed her mother and Melody, her mentor and mother figure.

"Was Devon ever violent?"

Libby thought for a few seconds. "I don't remember that about him. But I didn't know him well enough to say." The full-bodied fragrance of vanilla cake baking filled the room. I almost salivated. This would be the topping. She smeared the green icing into a pastry bag fitted with a leaf-piping tip. I never tired of watching her build cake art. The high school's order specified a welcome sign to staff and leaves in fall colors. She said she pictured the design in her mind and then sketched it out. It made the actual decorating go so much faster. Watching her execute the agonizing control it took to form this sugared sculpture was inspiring. She practiced the design on parchment paper and inspected it. Then a small fit of annoyance, she wadded it up and tossed it in the garbage.

Too bad I didn't have a creative bone in my body. I'd

learn, but there wouldn't be a need for it. I wouldn't be here forever. And she was teaching Marie her techniques. I'd never approach the skill level of Libby or Marie.

I did, however, have a discerning mind. Outlines surrounding Reginald Bateau's life were being filled in. Like one of Libby's sketches, Reginald's life was taking on color and texture in my imagination. As I wasn't privy to Bishop PD's investigation, I had to approach his murder from a different perspective. Finding out about Reginald's life might lead to his murderer. I hoped to have information to take to the chief, Frank Scherwin. Frank and I had formed a tenuous respect for each other over the romance of his son, Cameron, and Libby. If Frank had been in town, I was sure Sergeant Foster wouldn't have been so badge-heavy.

Chapter Twelve

I locked the Layers back door and whistled for Rusty. He'd gone around the corner to fertilize the weeds. I was tired from the emotion of the day. The shame of being accused of murder in public made me avoid people. How could this happen? I hadn't done anything wrong.

Then there was the new project I'd agreed to. I needed some computer time to organize a plan. This was new territory to me. I'd start from scratch, but for help, I'd rely on the Internet and the chamber.

Dogs were my safe place. I called Rusty once more. I heard his clicking toenails and opened the back door of my Camry. I really needed to think about finding another car before winter came. Rusty ran to me, not jumping up, thankfully. Behind him trotted Arco, the most beautiful German shepherd ever.

I sang out his name, "Arco." Happy to see him, I knew his handler and the man I dreamed about would follow. A double delight.

And unexpected. Jake wasn't due until this weekend.

Jake turned the corner, looking ahead for Arco and

me. The smile that spread across his face broke the lines of fatigue. Or maybe it had been worry. It didn't matter. He was here, and I was happy.

Jake wrapped his big arms around me and nuzzled my neck. "I'm so glad to be here."

"You must've left early."

He mumbled in my hair. "Five a.m."

I pulled away to search his face. He'd been scheduled to work the swing shift last night, which would've put him off duty at two o'clock in the morning. "Did you get any sleep?"

"An hour or two. It took some time and fancy talking to get someone to work my shift tonight."

We stood at my car. I pulled away. "You didn't need to be here. I'm perfectly fine."

"I know you are, Sarah. Only…"

"You are concerned about me." I faced him with my hand on my hip. "There's no need. I'm not in any danger, and no one is going to arrest me."

"Not sure about the 'no danger' part, but I know that no one is going to arrest you."

I stared at his bloodshot eyes. "You need a nap. Come out to my house and crash on the couch for an hour. Then, we'll talk."

He glanced at his wristwatch and agreed. "Are your folks still out of town?"

"'Til Tuesday morning."

"Any chance I can meet with Kelly at your house?"

I took his hand. "Of course." Besides my father and Wesley, these were the two men I trusted most in my life. It looked like I would put it in their hands again.

Chapter Thirteen

Rusty pawed the back door to go out. I must've been really engrossed in my festival notes because he never has to tell me to open the door. Earlier, I'd made a pot of coffee and two sandwiches for Jake. I had a snack as I hadn't eaten this morning. I'd let him sleep for another ten minutes, then wake him. Coffee and food would help him sharpen up for the meeting with Kelly. I opened the door and walked into the living room to signal Arco for a potty break.

Jake stood at the coffeemaker, pouring a cup when I came back in with the dogs. We'd affectionately nick-named them, 'the boys.'

"I hope the boys and I didn't wake you."

"I didn't really sleep much." I knew he'd slept better than he thought. One of the several times I checked on him, he was snoring. It was a light snore, not a heavy guttural noise. I smiled to myself when I decided it wouldn't bother me.

"The sandwiches are for you. I figured you must've

been in a hurry to get here and didn't take the time to stop."

He munched roast beef on rye and smiled his answer.

I cleared my throat. Finally, the right time had come. Although I dreaded a negative answer, I had to ask. "Has the chief made his decision about Arco?" With Jake's promotion to lieutenant, his position as a K-9 handler wasn't open anymore. Arco's advancing age made it difficult to transition to another handler for the year left before his retirement. Jake had petitioned to buy him from the city, and the chief was mulling it over.

"He's still considering it because Arco's so healthy. Retirement age is one more year, but..." Jake spread his hands in an anything-goes gesture.

I put my hand on his shoulder and kissed the top of his head. "I'm praying he sells this old guy to you." There wasn't any more to be said to him. But they were the perfect pair. Arco knew Jake's every mood, every nuance of his body language. If it came down to it, I thought Jake wouldn't be able to send Arco into a potentially deadly situation. At least, now, while in limbo, that wouldn't occur. Lieutenants don't deploy as K-9 officers in Petaluma.

When the last of the dishes were put away, I heard Kelly's knock at the front door. Jake answered, and the two men gave each other a hearty greeting. I'd envisioned the meeting to be in the living room, but the men wandered into the kitchen and pulled out chairs at the table.

Jake opened the subject by asking, "Kelly, have you heard any rumors from Bishop PD that might help? I mean, we know Sarah had nothing to do with Bateau's murder."

"Right, of course," Kelly said. He sat back in the

chair, fingering the handle of the half-full coffee mug in front of him. "They aren't talking. Mitch Foster is in charge of the investigation because the detective—they only have one—was out with pneumonia. Foster's in over his head. He's grasping at any easy answers he can find."

"Like tagging me the killer?"

Jake shook his head in amazement. "If he doesn't know what he's doing, why doesn't he ask for help from the sheriff's office?"

Kelly shrugged. "His ego would be my first guess."

"No ideas about the cause of death, weapon, or anything?"

"They're assuming the knife was from the kitchen, and I did hear there aren't any prints on it. As far as cause, I think we can believe the knife nicked an artery or hit the heart."

"Assuming anything in an investigation is a mistake." Jake plopped his coffee mug on the table, sloshing the contents. "Why didn't the employees call the cops?"

Kelly snorted. "Most of them are Mexican, and none of them trust the cops." He squinted an eye at me. "I heard that Foster tried to get a search warrant for your car and house, but the judge wouldn't go for it."

Digesting this information, Jake straightened and focused on me. "That's a point on the plus side for you. If a judge wouldn't sign a search warrant for your property, that means the jurist doesn't believe there's enough probable cause to think you were a party to the homicide."

"That is good news." Having Jake there, I was never in doubt. And this was why, he came up with perspectives I wouldn't have seen. I'm not sure Kelly would've seen Jake's angle either.

"Did Foster say why he questioned you so hard?" Kelly rubbed his crew-cut head, still trying to understand Bishop PD's reasoning.

"He said I had a motive." I rounded up his words in the soup sandwich that whirled around in my brain. "He said because Reg is the guy who incapacitated Melody, enabling another to finish her off. Two, I had opportunity —I had no one to verify my alibi after I left the sporting goods store. Foster said the murder would have taken two seconds for the stabbing and five for the 'decorations.'" I mimicked his crooked finger around the last word.

"What did he mean, 'decorations'?" Jake looked from Kelly to me.

I was uncomfortable explaining about the embellishments, but Jake should know. He was in a position to see matters of importance that I wouldn't deem significant. "The killer took a pastry bag—it was probably lying around. Javier said Reginald had kicked all the employees out." I took a breath. "The pastry bag full of icing with a number twenty-one tip on it. He squeezed some of it in Reginald's nose and mouth. In shapes. Stars for the eyes and nose, and a row of rosettes in his mouth. The icing filled his mouth and nose, and if he didn't die from the stab wounds, the icing could've suffocated him."

Jake's eyes widened. He glanced at Kelly, who didn't look shocked at all, then back to me.

"But from the few seconds I saw him, it didn't look like he breathed in any... material."

"Holy cow," Jake said. "When you said icing in his mouth, I couldn't have imagined. That's plain weird."

Kelly's head bobbed up and down. "Who would do that?"

Jake brought us back to center. "Is that the only reason he's looking at you?"

"Uh, no." Wondering how I was going to prove myself, I marched onward to the truth. "He said I had opportunity."

Kelly looked annoyed. "What?"

"Can you account for all your time?"

"Pretty much."

Chapter Fourteen

I t was Jake's turn to look annoyed. "How about a yes or no, Sarah."

"Would a timeline of that part of my day help?" Knowing that this would be important to help them form a picture in their minds, I'd typed and printed it out.

I handed Jake the sheet of paper with a chunk of my life on it.

Timeline:

- *11:00 a.m. - Mark showed up at Layers*
- *11:10 a.m. - I got a call from Javier at Boulangerie saying Reginald has lost it*
- *11:10-11:15a.m. - I arranged for Charlie to take over the front counter*
- *11:18 a.m. - I was blocked in the parking lot and finally left at 11:40*
- *11:45 a.m. - I arrived at Boulangerie and found Reginald's body; called 911*
- *11:50 a.m. - Police on scene*

- *12:00 p.m. - I go to police station for statement, and more questions per Sergeant Foster*
- *1:00 p.m. - Finally "released"*

Jake looked up at me. "Who's Mark?"

"Melody's brother." Kelly answered.

Jake's eyes narrowed. "Brother? I didn't know she had a brother. I don't remember hearing about him."

"There's a reason for that. More later," I promised. I was sure Kelly had heard of Mark's history. It was impossible for anyone living in Bishop in 2011 to not know. "Let's get on with the timeline."

Jake gave a half-shrug and moved on. "Let's look at times between the time you got Javier's call until you arrived when someone could get to Reginald."

"Mark showed up, and we talked until Javier called. I checked my call log, and the time I answered was eleven-ten. We spoke for less than a minute."

Kelly got up and poured us all another cup of coffee. "What did you do after that?"

"I had to get someone to cover the front counter, so I pulled Charlie from the kitchen. It took me a few minutes to teach him about the register and closing at the end of the day. I had no idea how long I'd be."

Kelly sat down with a thump. "That makes sense. Reginald is high-maintenance, and you two have a bit of a track record."

"I went outside and found a van blocking my car. Using my superior powers of deduction, I went to the sports shop across the street. Sure enough, one of the rock climbers owned the van. It took a few minutes for him to get his pants on and..."

I stopped with a laugh at both their faces. "He was in the dressing room."

Jake smiled with relief at the explanation. Kelly laughed outright.

I continued. "By eleven-forty, I pulled out of the parking lot. I checked the clock on my car dashboard. It took me five minutes to get to Boulangerie at eleven forty-five. I walked to the front door, and it was locked with the *closed* sign hung up. I walked around back, and the kitchen door was open. Once inside, there was no one around, though I wasn't expecting anyone but Reginald. Javier said he'd fired everyone and booted them out."

Kelly shook his head at Reginald's behavior.

"I found him on the floor." I paused, collecting my memories. "It was a shock to see him dead. And with the icing... anyway, I called 911 at eleven forty-seven a.m. I can't say when the police got there, but it felt like forever."

"I looked it up. It was three minutes." Kelly drank the last of his coffee.

"I don't know." Jake shook his head. "This is a very tight timeline. I can't believe this sergeant can see where your opportunity was."

I agreed. "Olive was at OVS, the sporting goods store, and saw me asking about the owner of a white van. She should be able to vouch for the time."

"What about other ways of proving your timeline? Did you see anyone you know? Wave to them? Maybe businesses with closed-circuit cameras? Banks, gas stations?"

Kelly spoke up. "The Owens Valley Bank has cameras, but I can't say for sure if they'll be focused on Main Street. Traffic cams are useless. Caltrans hasn't downloaded them for months, probably years. I had a pursuit through town last year, and the DA tried to subpoena the film, but it was a non-starter."

"Bishop Museum has one. It's right across the street from the Boulangerie. I remember seeing it yesterday. Who knows what it's aimed at—Main Street or the parking lot? I'll check on that tomorrow."

"No, you won't." Jake held up his hand, ever the traffic cop. "You go to work like you always do. I'll check. I'm here for the next three days."

Startled at the sound of an order, I protested. "Now, wait a minute. You don't tell me…"

He put a gentle hand on mine, stopping my opposition. "I'm sorry I sounded like a drill sergeant. I'm concerned about you and your safety. Remember what happened last spring when you did all that snooping?"

Yeah, we caught a killer, was on the tip of my tongue, but I didn't say it. He was right, as much as I hated to admit it.

I should be careful. The killer is still out there.

Chapter Fifteen

Kelly stood. "We have some checking to do. It's better than sitting here waiting for Foster to come arrest Sarah." He rinsed his coffee mug in the sink. "I've got to get to work. We'll check in later?"

Jake rose and shook his hand. "Thanks, bud. I'm happy to have local help."

I walked Kelly to the door while Jake cleaned up the dishes. "Thanks for everything, Kelly. I don't think we could've done without you."

He waved the thought away with a half smile and left.

"We're lucky to have him on our team." Jake settled into the sofa, Arco at his feet.

Rusty wasn't nearly as well-mannered. He'd hopped on the sofa and draped himself across my lap, his head touching Jake's lap. He snuck a long pink tongue out and licked Jake. Jake smiled and asked, "Is that what we are— a team?" The thought amused me.

His brown eyes searched until they caught my gaze. With a finger scratching Rusty's ear, his voice was soft.

"You know what I mean." He leaned in and kissed me gently on the lips.

It felt good. It felt right. But I worried that I might be holding him back from another opportunity. He'd said he'd wait for me. Ghosts from my previous marriage had diminished over the summer, but I wondered if I'd ever be ready for another *real* relationship. I wrestled with my feelings because I didn't want this man to get away. He was more than I could ask for in a partner. But what did he want for his future?

"Jake, tell me how you see the rest of your life. I mean, your career, your relationships, your father." I couldn't meet his eyes. I didn't want to influence his answer.

"Simple answer?" He used a finger to turn my chin. He stared into my eyes, exactly what I'd been avoiding. My stomach flipped. "I want you in my future. I want to come home every day from work to hear about your day. I want to tell you about my day. I want kids running around underfoot."

I sighed and pictured this blissful scene. It's what I wanted too. "It sounds like heaven. But there were more futures in my question. What are your career goals?"

"I thought I told you. I like being a lieutenant, for now. I'd like to make chief someday. But if that doesn't happen, I'm happy as a lieutenant. I've already made it farther than I thought I would."

That sounded a bit dark. "Did you doubt yourself? Your abilities?"

"No. I always knew I could lead. I was a pretty good street cop, but leading is a different skill set. Especially these days when every move a cop makes is videotaped and second-guessed. In some cases, it helps with transparency, but it also makes cops defensive and afraid. That's an ugly mix in dogs and cops."

"Why do you say you've made it farther than you thought you would?"

"My father is an attorney. Didn't I tell you that?" At my nod, he went on. "He's a tax attorney, retired now. He wanted me to follow him in business and eventually take over the practice. I resisted, and we butted heads. He's still angry that both his sons found different paths than him." Jake turned his head, and there was irony in his smile. "He knows what's best for his sons, and he's always right. Just ask him."

I laughed. "I can't see you or Wesley as tax attorneys."

He chuckled. "Your turn. What about your dreams?"

"Gosh. They've changed so much within this past year. But I think I'm getting a handle on what I want out of life." Kids? Since talking to Emily, I couldn't stop thinking about children of my own. But it was too soon to decide about that. Wasn't it? Gee, I was thirty-six years old. How much time did I have? Jake didn't need to know about this—yet.

"Okay." Jake drew out the word and rolled his hand to encourage me to continue.

"First, I want to keep Layers on its current path. We're becoming profitable enough that I've been able to pay salaries to everyone. We've put some money back into the business, but most of the profit has gone to Wesley, as it should."

"He told me you'd sent some money his way." Jake took my hand. "What else?"

"The other part of that dream is actually Melody's. I want to take the nonprofit and shape it into a full-fledged program for kids on the fence of good or bad futures."

"That's one of the things I love about you, Sarah. You think of others before yourself. You've talked about Better Off Baking before. So what about you? What do you want?"

"Like I don't already have enough to do, I got wrangled into organizing a Fall Colors Festival in five weeks here in town."

Jake blinked, then shook his head in disbelief.

I explained the project, including my own rationalizations for agreeing. Finally, I said, "It's only for the next five weeks, and I plan on delegating as much as possible."

When I expected a protest, he said, "I can hear the excitement in your voice, Sarah. This sounds like a great project for you. But it's tough timing."

"The main fundraiser is for a local nonprofit that provides vet care for injured animals. If anyone else had found Arco four months ago…" Arco heard his name, and his tail thumped against the couch. "…this group would've paid for his medical care until the owner showed up."

"A good cause, for sure." He rubbed his eyes with the heels of his hands, then picked up my hand. "You must have other goals. Care to share?" He smiled at the rhyme.

"Short term, I'm planning on working Javier into Layers's new manager. I'd really like to go back to work in court. I love that job."

"I'll bet you're good at it too." He traced my ear in a touch so gentle it felt like a butterfly wing had touched me. His other hand gripped mine in a velvet-soft hold.

"I hope so."

"Okay. Where do you see us going?"

I took in a deep breath. "When I moved here, my

plans were simple—get the reporting job, heal from my divorce, and buy a house—not in any special order."

The coffee-colored eyes blinked as if it cleared his mind. His face held no expression at all. He was waiting. He'd heard a short version of this before. We'd talked about our dreams early in our relationship.

"But then I met you, and it all changed." My heart thudded in my chest. I felt the risk I would soon take, and it wasn't easy. "I'm falling in love with you, Jake. I know it and can't do a thing about it." I sniffed to give myself time to find the right words. "I want you for a husband, to make a home with." I loved how his eyes brightened. "And dogs." I scratched Rusty's ear again. I knew dogs would be in our future. I wanted to say, and kids, too, but I wasn't sure. I thought I wanted babies, but I wasn't sure enough to say it.

Jake held my hand to his heart. "Then we're on the same path. I don't have to worry about you running back to your ex in LA or anything."

"Oh no. What an awful thought."

"But for the moment, we will take it slow, the way you want it." He grimaced as he released my hand in my lap. "And we need to get this murder investigation out of the way."

"Yes, we do." I was strangely pleased at the 'we' he used.

Chapter Sixteen

A car pulled into the driveway, and I suddenly remembered. "Oh no, I'm sorry I forgot." I stood and glanced out the front window. "I invited your brother to dinner tonight."

Jake's smile was so gentle and serene, you'd have thought I'd promised him heaven. "Two of my favorite people on earth together—how could that need an apology?"

At the door, Wesley stood rocking with laughter, his hands behind him. "You forgot, didn't you?"

"I did." I felt the heat coloring my face. "I'm so sorry."

"Lucky for you, I know you so well." He twisted an arm and presented me with a wonderfully fragrant extra-large pizza box. "For all your sensibleness, Sarah, when you have matters like a murder investigation on your mind, you forget details like dinner."

I motioned him inside. Rusty scampered around us, excited to have another person to adore him. And maybe drop some of the wonderful-smelling food on the floor.

"Jake, glad you could make it." Wesley nodded at his brother, who trailed us into the kitchen.

I pulled out plates and napkins to set the table. Both boys shook their heads, no, for forks, but I set one for myself. I filled drink orders—beer for Wesley, merlot for Jake and me—and sat down. I was starved. I'd only had a snack today and was ready for dinner. How could I have forgotten dinner? Passing the parmesan cheese, I asked Wesley, "Have you heard from Mark?"

Wesley snorted into his beer glass. He grimaced when he put it down. "Yeah. He's at a buddy's house right now and will be at home by nine."

"Will it be tough to have him around?" I thought how much Mark looked like Melody. How his gestures—when he dismissed matters that he didn't care about—were so like his sister. And he'll be asking tough questions.

Wesley chewed thoughtfully. "Yes. I'm hoping it'll be a short visit."

To Jake, I asked, "Have you met him yet?"

Jake nodded, seeming to search for the right words. "Yeah, I stopped at Wes' place before I came to see you." He put his wineglass down. "I have to admit, he didn't make a good first impression."

"It's tough to see someone who you know has caused so much heartbreak in his family." Wes swirled his brew. "Melody loved him, but she wasn't blind to the damage he'd done to Tom and Anna."

"Anyone care to enlighten me? Or is this not a good time?"

I finished my piece of pizza and wiped my hands. "There will never be a good time to tell Mark Gibson's story." With a glance at Wesley, I began. "I'll start, and you can pick up the later years."

At Wesley's nod, I launched into the ugly story.

"Mark's three years older than Melody and me. He was always a bad boy, even as a kid. My first memories of him were of his father yelling for him to stop doing something. But he had an innate magnetism that made people gravitate to him. He was handsome—a beautiful child who relied on his charm and looks to get his way. Usually, on the sly, he did things that got him in trouble. He'd climb out his bedroom window at night and smoke and drink. As he got older, in high school, he partied a lot. Then he... uh... got a girl in trouble."

Wesley picked up the story. "He'd barely turned sixteen and refused to marry the girl. He shirked his responsibility, leaving the girl to fend for herself. Abortion was out of the question because of the family's religious beliefs. Her parents didn't know how to deal with the problem. They were at a loss and made the only choice they could. They kicked her out, and life became unbearable for her. The Gibsons were arranging to take her in, but Mark delayed it. Can you imagine having a pregnant teen in your home with the father denying any responsibility? Mark was relentless in his denial."

Wesley drank the last of his beer. "The search and rescue folks found her body in the canal outside of town after two days. They called it an accidental drowning. There was no way of knowing whether she committed suicide or not."

"Her parents blamed Mark, even though they were the ones who had turned her out." The memory of those days of turmoil wrenched at my heart. They were dark times. Mom and Dad debated Mark's dilemma and failed to come up with a solution. Tom and Anna were brokenhearted. "I didn't know the girl, but any death as pointless as hers was excruciating to the entire community. Her folks lived right outside of town and pressured friends and neighbors to shun the Gibsons, especially Mark."

Jake's eyes widened. "Shun? Like in the Bible?"

I nodded while Wesley finished the story. "The Gibsons are great people with a long Owens Valley history. His ancestors were pioneers who arrived here during the Civil War and raised cattle and horses. There are a lot of folks around here who depended on the Gibsons through the years. Packers, cowboys, agriculture, and such. They're local royalty."

Jake looked at me. "Your mom?"

Wesley nodded. "Yeah, she's Tom's sister. But in the end, the girl's family couldn't take it. The shame and their awkward way of dealing with it soured them. They tried to get people to shun the Gibsons for what their son had done, and it backfired. They moved to Reno within a year of her death."

"What about Mark?" Jake's scowl made it seem he didn't really want to know.

Wesley was in college by then, but I was around. I'd been there for some of the arguments. Wesley looked at me.

"Mark couldn't make a go of it in Bishop, either. This wasn't the entire reason, as he was already on a bad path. But it was the breaking point for him. He barely graduated from high school and wasn't college material. He was too full of himself to consider a trade, so he left. He never even said goodbye to his parents."

Wesley added his last comments. "Melody loved her brother despite all the problems he had. After a few years, he phoned her, and they stayed in touch. Sometimes years went by without hearing from him, but she always prayed for him."

There was silence at the table while Jake digested the

story, and Wesley and I remembered. The fact that Mark was in the same class as Reginald and Judith wafted through my memory but didn't strike a chord.

"A tragic story," Jake whispered. Then, glancing from Wesley to me, he asked, "The question is, what is he doing here now? To find out what happened to his sister? He could've accomplished that with a phone call."

I had no answer, neither did Wesley.

Chapter Seventeen

The next day, I suggested Emily meet me at Layers. I didn't usually take coffee breaks, but when Emily and I talked about catching up, I thought this might be more private than a coffee shop or restaurant. The upstairs office was small and crowded with boxes of supplies, but two chairs and a desk fit inside snugly. Rusty moved out to the landing and resumed his nap.

Tiffani, our new barista, practiced on us with her pumpkin spice lattes. We carried them upstairs and settled into a catch-up gabfest. She had married a decent man, Matt Kilbride, and now had four kids, two dogs, and three cats. And one horse. "I work to pay for hay, vets, and farriers." Her broad smile revealed a mustache of latte cream on her upper lip. She'd put on a few pounds since high school, but they looked good on her. She beamed health and happiness. I vowed silently to keep in touch. She was as honest and true a friend as there was.

She pushed the empty latte mug away and used a ring finger to blot sugar crumbs from a cruller. She licked the sugar off her finger. "Tell me about this program you have. My sister's kid is interested."

"It's not my program. Melody started it."

"I'm so sorry about her passing, Sarah." Emily's mouth twisted in a sympathetic pout. "I know how close you were." She reached across the desk and grasped my hand.

I squeezed it in return, then stirred my latte. "You met Libby downstairs?" At her nod, I continued. "Melody mentored Libby when she was a juvenile with a bad attitude, wobbling on the fence of reckless, criminal behavior or dependable adulting. Because of the trust Melody put in Libby, she is now the head baker at Layers, responsible for menu planning, organizing labor, as well as baking. She's taking college classes at Cerro Coso Community College with an eye on the hospitality industry. She's shaping into a leadership role for the young kids like her. In short, she has a future, no matter how tough her today is, tomorrow is way more promising."

"Wow, that's an inspirational story."

"All true, Em." There was more, and Emily had the patience to listen. "Here's the news about the nonprofit —we're calling it BOB, which stands for Better Off Baking."

"Catchy." Emily grinned.

I took a deep breath. "The paperwork is all finalized under the new name. We even have a board of directors: Wesley, Tom, Anna Gibson, and my folks, Meg and Rob Murray. So it's for real."

"What do you mean, for real? Explain."

"Last spring, Libby and I picked a few students from her continuation school who were interested in learning baking skills. We narrowed it down to two kids who worked with us for five weeks. Into summer, actually, after school ended. They liked it so much that one plans to come back with us this year. The other has gone on to Cerro Coso College and is working at a Bishop Creek restaurant in the kitchen. We haven't yet started this semester's group, and three is our max due to the small quarters."

"Have you picked this semester's kids yet?"

"We've got it down to six at the moment. We'll pick two more. We'll finalize the selection next week." I pushed my empty mug aside. "Tell me about your sister's son."

Emily talked for fifteen minutes straight about her nephew, Austin. His story could've been Libby's, with the differences only in the minor details. It sounded like her nephew had the drive to improve himself and had a love for the mysteries of the kitchen. She gave me his phone number, and I said, "I'll get hold of him soon and put him in the running. Libby is instrumental in making the decisions, too, so I'll need to schedule a meeting around her." It was only reasonable to give her a hand in the selections. After all, she was the head baker and would be spending time teaching these kids. Emily didn't need to know about the expansion I planned. I'd save that for another coffee break, hopefully in Layers' newly renovated front counter area with four tables and chairs.

We ended our coffee break with a quick hug. She had to get to work, and so did I. It was payroll time. Yuck.

Maybe I'd take a spin up Main Street to Bishop Museum instead.

Chapter Eighteen

I left Rusty in the office while I went on my expedition. I drove down Main Street, past City Park. I slowed at Park Street and pulled into the lot at Bishop Museum. It was ten thirty, toward the end of summer, and getting hotter by the minute. There was only one car in the parking lot, running, with the air conditioner on and a beautiful German shepherd in the back seat.

I should've known that Jake would beat me there. He'd parked his white SUV on the right side under the sign. It was like he knew I'd show up and wanted me to know he was on the job. I smiled to myself, wondering how I could be so lucky to have found him.

Inside, he stood at the far side of the front door, leaning on a planter and sipping on a water bottle. As I walked to him, he gave me the lopsided grin that I was coming to love. "Been here long?" If I knew him, he'd been there for hours, waiting, believing that I'd show up.

He shrugged. "Want some water? There's some in the car."

I shook my head and pulled the door open. We found

an adult-sized table and sat while he finished off his drink. I couldn't stand it any longer. "Well? Did you ask about a camera?"

He laughed, a wonderful sound, even though it was at my expense. "They had a camera, and it's still set up. The manager didn't know if it ever worked, but it doesn't now. That didn't stop someone from shooting it up on Tuesday morning."

"That's when the murder occurred." I shook my head. "No one heard anything?"

The manager said some kids came in to report it to them. They said they didn't want to get blamed, but they probably did it or know who did. The owner climbed up and found some BBs. They could've been what did the damage."

"It's too bad. It's in the optimum position to film activity at Boulangerie right across the street." I glanced around. "What about the visitor center? It wouldn't catch a person entering from the back but..."

"Already checked. No cameras."

I sighed. I'd been found out. I was a snoop. I couldn't resist, and Jake had busted me. "This was a wasted trip." I started to get up when he put his hand on my wrist.

"Wait."

Oh no. Here it comes. I tried to look innocent. "What?"

He rubbed his face with both hands. He looked frustrated. "Look. I know I'm never gonna convince you to stop poking around. But will you please take someone along from now on? At least I'll have some peace of mind that you'll be in less danger with another person along."

It was a reasonable request, given the circumstances. "Okay." I knew I'd evaluate each situation on its individual merits—or demerits. A simple okay should appease him. And he'd asked nicely. The glimmer of concern kindled in me about his overprotectiveness. I'd file that away and revisit it from time to time. I hope it didn't ignite into control. "Did you get some sleep last night?"

He eyed me for a second, then agreed to the change in subjects. "Yeah. I was tired. Nothing could've kept me away, even Mark and Wesley arguing."

"Uh-oh."

"Yep. I don't like that guy. I know he's your cousin, but he does what he pleases and doesn't care how it affects others. Arco doesn't like him either."

"Mark is difficult, for sure." I stood, anxious to get away from talking about my troublesome cousin. "I need to get back to work. I have payroll to do."

He rose and kissed me on the cheek. "See you later? Text me when you're finished with work and can have company."

I couldn't stop smiling as we left, and I walked to his car with him. When he opened the door, Arco stuck his wet pointy nose in mine. I'd fallen for this old boy long before I met his handler. I ruffled the fur on his neck and said goodbye.

Chapter Nineteen

At Layers, I heard yelling as I walked through the back door.

I called out. "Libby?"

"This is crap." Frustrated with the quality of the flour lately, Libby slammed a bag on the worktable. I knew she cussed, but never around me. Melody had established that rule in the first days at the bakery. I merely continued it. Still, it was unusual for her to yell. The kitchen was separated from the front counter area by a door, so customers could hear a commotion in the back. She knew better.

"Libby?" We needed to talk about this. Marie, the mouse, cowered next to a shelf under the stairs. This wasn't good.

"Sarah." she wailed. With a red face and swollen, damp eyes, she walked into my arms. Sobbing, she swayed back and forth, searching for comfort.

It was then I remembered today was the first day of her father's sentencing. She'd taken the opportunity to speak to the judge about the loss of her mother, then ten years later, the loss of her mentor, Melody. I kicked myself for not standing by her during this difficult time.

"Marie, take over here, please. Finish whatever she started." The baking assistant crept to the worktable as I scooped Libby and pushed her upstairs. Rusty had trotted halfway down, then scampered back up when he saw us.

I steered Libby to the chair opposite mine at the desk. She leaned her head onto her crossed arms on the desk. I placed a box of tissues at her elbow and let her cry as I stroked her purple hair. I should've been in court with her. She'd told me she'd be fine with Cameron, her boyfriend, beside her. But I should've been there.

After five minutes, she ran out of tears. On the verge of hyperventilating, I had her drop her head between her knees. I stroked her back, continuing to offer what belated comfort I could.

Soon, she settled down. I was as close as she had to family besides her father. Cameron and Libby were close, but he was still young and inexperienced in trauma such as she'd lived. I felt it was down to me.

She straightened and twisted a tissue. "It was worse than I could imagine, Sarah."

I couldn't say a word. I had to let her talk.

"He sat there in the courtroom next to his attorney and didn't even look at me. When I talked about my loss, I saw his shoulders shake. But I couldn't tell if he was crying or laughing. Finally, I said what I had to say to the judge. Then I left."

"Cameron?"

Her head shook. "He was there, but I think I scared him on the way home. I was crying, and he didn't know what to do. He took me home first, but I couldn't be there. I had to come here. This is my only safe place."

Her home held the staircase where her father pushed her mother to her death. Libby hadn't been aware of the truth until recently. She and her father lived in that house for ten years.

I thought about how sad it was that this was her safe place. It was here that Libby got the first taste of respect and trust. Melody provided that and changed Libby's life. Then her father had killed Melody when he believed Libby had told her the truth. The irony was that Libby didn't even recall the details of that night until four months ago—when Grant Armstrong plotted to kill me for the same reason.

"Yes, Libby. You'll always be safe here."

She sighed deeply, and for the first time, I saw something flickering in her eyes. The beginnings of hope. Hope for a better future and the courage to make it happen.

Chapter Twenty

L ibby and I walked downstairs. She apologized to Marie for her temper without giving a reason. She wouldn't want anyone to share the burden she carried, other than Cameron and me. Libby walked outside in the bright fall sunlight with me to watch Rusty do his business. She chatted like a weight had been lifted.

Maybe it had. The purpose of victim impact statements is to help the judge hear how a criminal action has affected the victim. A side effect is that it helps the victim close the door on the tragedy suffered at the hands of the defendant. It seemed to have made a difference to Libby.

"Have you heard any more about Reggie-baby's murder?"

"Libby, that's so disrespectful of a dead person. It's Reginald."

She shrugged. "He'll always be Reggie-baby because he didn't deserve my respect while he was alive, and certainly not now that somebody's offed him."

"To answer the question, no. Jake's here, and we've

eliminated our last lead." We walked back inside. Marie had put a tray of blueberry muffins in an oven and spoke quietly to a young man beside her. I continued telling Libby the most current news. "We had hoped the Bishop Museum camera across from Boulangerie would record a person or significant movement. But it had been vandalized, so we couldn't get anything."

"Vandalized?"

"Someone shot the camera out with BBs. Turns out the camera wasn't working anyway, so it's definitely a dead end."

At the worktable, Libby and I took up our usual positions. Only, she wasn't working today. "Marie, who's your friend?"

Marie's face reddened at the question. "Oh, uh. This is Austin. He's interested in the internship, and Charlie let him in to watch."

Emily's nephew. "Austin, nice to meet you." I extended a hand and got a firm handshake back. "This is Libby, the head baker, and I'm Sarah Murray, the manager."

Austin gave a shy smile. "My aunt said she knows you."

"Yes, we had coffee together just this morning."

He flashed a toothy smile. "I know. She said."

"Did she tell you I'd contact you for an interview?"

"Yeah. I mean, yes." He sobered.

"We can make the appointment right now." I looked at Libby, who gave me a shrug.

We set a time for tomorrow when Libby and I would be free to spend a half hour talking to this young man. He certainly showed initiative being here.

But now I had payroll to do.

"Uh, Miz Murray." Austin followed me to the stairs.

"Before, when you and Miz Armstrong came downstairs, you were talking about the camera at the museum."

"Yes? What about it?" What was this about?

His voice lowered like he was going to tell a secret. "I was there when the camera got shot out."

"What?"

"Me and some friends were hanging out, and some guy came over and shot it out with a BB gun. We was standing right there. It was like we wasn't even there. He hid over by the Bishop Museum sign. Maybe he didn't even see us."

I collected my thoughts, tying threads together. "What time was it?"

"The fire siren went off at ten o'clock. I checked my phone and noticed the time. That's what it read."

"In the morning? Ten o'clock?" I couldn't believe my ears. This could mean Reginald's death was premeditated.

At his nod, I had to push further. "Do you know who he was? Have you seen him before?"

"Nah."

"Could you identify him if you saw him?"

Austin looked at the ceiling and thought. "I think so. He was kind of tall and skinny looking."

"Will you go to the police with this information? It could be important."

His hands flew out to block the possibility. "No way. I uh... No way."

Deflated but still energized, I told him thanks and sent him on his way. I'd have to figure out how to convince him to come forward.

Chapter Twenty-One

Dinner was at the McLaren house. The parents were still gone, and Jake wasn't anxious to spend time with Mark, who was still at Wesley's. I'd fixed an easy dinner of lemon chicken and brought home a cherry pie for dessert from Layers.

Jake patted his stomach after pushing away the empty plate with crumbs from his piece of pie. "I'm going to have to take up running if you cook any more for me."

"The dinner was easy, and the pie even easier. I brought it from the bakery. Libby made it."

"Is she single?"

I tossed a dish towel at him. "For that remark, you're helping with dishes."

"We can't do a photo lineup to ID the guy who shot out the camera."

"Right. I thought so. Don't you need pictures of the bad guy and five similar types?"

"Yes, but we don't know who he is. We learn who he is, then we can do a photo lineup for a formal identification."

"So, where are we going to find a picture for Austin to look at?"

"The newspaper?" The *Inyo Register*.

"No, it comes out once a week, and it would be really good luck to contain his photo."

"Not good luck for him." There was that lopsided smile.

"Oh, I have an idea. What about a yearbook?" I still had mine—somewhere. And if the guy wasn't in any of my high school years, I could bring Austin to the library and go through their copies.

"Sure, if he's a local and his picture is in there."

I thought about where I'd buried my yearbooks. Which box? In the barn? A shed? The garage? Dad had tons of storage places. The barn wasn't used since I'd gone off to college, and my horse went to Tom and Anna's. Since Dad wasn't here, I'd have to sort through the property to find where he'd directed the movers to dump my worldly possessions.

Why hadn't I done this before? I'd been here almost four months. "I'll go look for my yearbooks. I don't know where the boxes are. They could be in the barn or a shed or the garage."

He put his hands up, signaling I'd said enough. "That's my cue to hit the trail. Guess I've put off going back to Wesley's long enough."

"Mark?"

He scowled in response.

I began a defense of my cousin, but the words didn't make sense. I finally admitted, "He is tough to be around, especially if you're an observer and not family. You're better off avoiding him, believe me."

Jake leaned over and kissed my lips. A caress, a whisper of silk, and a testament to how much he cared.

He straightened with a pained frown. "I feel like I need to say this once more, Sarah. Please be careful when you're asking people questions." He had more to say but stopped. His lips pursed in an expression that told me he'd said too much already.

I nodded, a tiny irritation growing in my chest as I said goodbye. Is he trying to control me? I'd had enough of that from Blaine and wanted no part of a partner who told me what to do. But darn it, he's so wonderful in every other way.

Rusty trotted alongside as I searched the outbuildings for my boxes. Hmm, I'll have to watch for Jake's tendency to control and see if I was being hypercritical or realistic.

Chapter Twenty-Two

I arrived the next morning at six thirty. I took Rusty upstairs, where he promptly dropped into his bed on the landing. I tucked my backpack and sweater under the desk and went downstairs.

Libby seemed refreshed and as relaxed as she gets. With three mixing bowls on the worktable, I saw she was in a serious baking mood. Good. Yesterday's cupcakes were history. She would replenish the supply with her chocolate chip, peanut butter blossoms, and sugar cookies—always a hit. Today, I noted the icing mix and food coloring nearby. I guessed the sugar cookies were getting a fall colors motif. My mouth watered at the thought. Marie worked on a sheet cake, and Charlie returned from the front counter with an empty tray. The cases had been stocked.

I thanked God for Libby's surprising work ethic and the two pairs of hands that helped behind the scenes, Marie and Charlie. Both had gifts to bring Melody's dream to fruition. Marie was painfully shy but got lost in cake recipes and decorations. Her red velvet cake was delicious and had been discovered by the locals. It was the leading sales item for birthdays and celebrations.

Charlie had excelled in breads. While his specialty was a deliciously moist cornbread, ordered specially for barbeque dinners, he showed the patience required for bread dough to be mixed, then kneaded, and the long time of rising. He also pitched in at the front counter when Anna was off, as she was this week. I looked forward to Halloween for Libby's cookies and Thanksgiving for Charlie's breads and rolls. And any day was a good day for Marie's cakes.

I heard the hiss of the milk frother from the espresso machine, which meant Tiffani had finally learned how to set an alarm on her phone. I poked my head around the corner to tell her good morning. She was too busy to reply.

A short line queued up for the fall special lattes: pumpkin spice, salted caramel, chai tea, maple cinnamon, apple spice, and maple sea salt. The aromas were intoxicating. I watched the breeze stir up leaves on the sidewalk outside and felt so blessed that I was home again. The weather was still warm, hot even, but forecasters predicted a cooling trend beginning next week. I could hardly wait. I loved the Eastern Sierras in the fall. The leaves changing daily from yellow to red, to brown, like a tableau of Mother Nature's color palette. And all refreshed by the cool mountain breezes.

I tied an apron on and went to help dish and bag pastries. A steady stream of customers kept Tiffani and me busy. I marveled at how adept she'd become at the espresso machine. When I worked it, I had to think through each step. My froth never looked as nice as hers. This darn machine was smarter than me.

At nine-thirty, the crowd had thinned enough for

Tiffani to take a break. She sure needed one after the busy morning. She strolled to the front door while scrolling through her phone. She bumped into a customer on his way in.

I frowned, thinking I might have to mention that to her, when I realized who the customer was—Mark. Thinking the worst of him, I expect that he bumped into the attractive young Tiffani on purpose. He gave me a knowing smile—and I had to wonder what it was he thought he *knew*. Mark needed to be special to everyone. He tried to present a special connection to those he met.

I didn't fall for it, but I said nothing beyond, "Good morning. Coffee?"

"Sure, if you're offering." He leaned his elbows on the counter in a revoltingly intimate way. He'd recently bordered on flirting with me, which I found repulsive. Sometimes I wondered how foolish I could've been to have loved my cousin. It also occurred to me that he'd look upon the coffee as free because I offered it. I sighed.

"How are things with you, cuz? I heard you and Blake broke up."

"Blaine."

"Whatever." He waved away the triviality of ten years of my life with a man named Blaine. "Do you have the keys to Mom and Dad's house?"

"I do."

He reached out a hand, long elegant fingers wiggling as they waited for the keys. "May I have them?"

"No." I only had a key for backup. Tom and Anna had a friend's daughter staying at their house, feeding the cats and chickens. No way would I facilitate my cousin barging in on her. Besides, I couldn't believe the Gibsons would allow him there. They didn't even acknowledge they had a son.

"Please." he whined in a patronizing tone.

"No. Your parents wouldn't want you there."

"You don't know that." He pulled away, straightening and glancing out the front window.

"Why do you want to stay there? What's wrong with Wesley's?" I had a suspicion.

Mark fished out a toothpick from the dispenser on the counter. He stuck it in his mouth.

"The Charters' house is not as cordial as I remember it being. Of course, Melody is gone, and that makes a difference. Wesley is okay. He's always been a bit superior, you know. College educated and a man of the cloth." He eyed me, looking for validation in my reaction.

I didn't give it to him. Wesley and I had grown closer since Melody's death. I felt more loyalty to him than ever. Maybe it had something to do with upholding Melody's own care for her husband. I'd honor it with my respect. Mark couldn't shake that.

He chewed the toothpick. "It's that other guy, his brother. He's an..."

I flashed a warning look.

"He's inhospitable, let's put it that way."

There wasn't a doubt in my mind that Jake was inhospitable.

"And that dog, he's a menace."

I wanted to shout at him then. I wanted to tell him that Arco had found his sister in the desert and tried to protect her. He'd gotten injured trying to save her. But the words would've bounced off him because they didn't further his agenda.

At that moment, I was so filled with disgust that I had to make him leave. There was only one thing to do. I poured him the dregs of coffee in a cardboard cup with a lid. "It's to go."

Cornbread

- 1 cup cornmeal
- 1 cup flour
- 4 tsp. baking powder
- 2 tbs. sugar
- 1 tsp. salt
- 2 eggs
- 1 cup milk
- ¼ cup canola oil

Blend eggs, milk, and oil. Stir in dry ingredients. Bake in a greased 8x8-inch pan at 425 degrees for 30 minutes or in a greased muffin tin for 20 minutes. Enjoy!

Chapter Twenty-Three

Tiffani returned moments later, blinking in the artificial light as the doorbell jingled. Mark had gotten my message and walked past her without moving out of her way. She almost bumped him again. I watched Mark walk out into the sunlight, slip on sunglasses with one hand, and taste the coffee. He sipped it, then flung it in the gutter.

With Tiffani back and no customers, I went back into the kitchen. Late mornings and afternoons weren't so busy in bakeries. But the kitchen was a hive of activity, mostly cleanup and prep for tomorrow. I passed through, went upstairs, and attached the leash to Rusty's collar. He needed a break as much as I did. Out the back door and into the parking lot, we'd found a small parkway across the street where Rusty could do his business on the grass.

While I stood waiting for Rusty, I played back the internal video of Mark's visit. I found myself getting angrier, so I had to distract myself. I glanced down the block and saw Austin.

Just who I needed to talk to. I waved him down, "Austin. Come here for a minute if you're not busy, please."

He sauntered up the sidewalk with a friend who shoved him a goodbye when he got close to me.

"I'd like you to help me with a task. Today if you can."

"Well, yeah. I have an interview with you in two hours."

Oh yes, now I remembered. "Can you come over now? I have a favor to ask."

His brows drew together. This was a major decision for him.

I bit. "I'll buy you lunch."

"Taco Bell?" He squinted, appearing to doubt that he could get the fine cuisine he wanted.

"Yes, whatever you want."

"All right. What do you want me to do? Move furniture?"

"No, easier than that." I tried to minimize what I would ask of him. "I'd like you to go through some yearbooks to see if you can find the guy who shot out the museum camera."

"Oh, man." His face scrunched like he wished he was going to move furniture.

"I'll put you at a table in the kitchen with coffee or a latte or whatever you want to drink and your lunch. You'll go through the yearbook page by page and look for this guy."

"Oh, man," he said again. "Three tacos with nachos, three chalupas, and a Pepsi."

I committed his order to memory and walked into the bakery with him. Rusty sat like a gentleman. He knew he wasn't allowed to roam in the kitchen, and he stayed by

my side as I jogged upstairs to retrieve the backpack and
yearbooks I'd put inside.

I got Austin started, had a word with Libby to tell her
where I was going, and set off to buy Austin his bribe—
er, lunch.

Chapter Twenty-Four

At two o'clock, I locked the front door. A man sprinted up and used a knuckle to knock on the glass. I pointed to the *closed* sign. He shook his head, signaling he didn't want anything from the bakery. I pointed an index finger at me, and he nodded.

What now?

I let him in, a man of my height and maybe ten years older than me. Pale brown curls shook when he nodded a thank you. The breeze blew in a few leaves. Darn, I'd just swept the floor.

"What can I do for you?" I had an ugly sensation in the pit of my stomach.

"Sarah Murray?" When I replied in the affirmative, he went on. "I'm Victor Rogers from Inyo County Schools."

I dreaded what would come next. "Okay."

"I'm here to tell you that the district has prohibited students to participate in your program, Better Off Baking. The course has been suspended until your role in the… um… homicide has been adjudicated or otherwise resolved."

I couldn't protest. I'd been half expecting something of the sort. I had no counter-argument. Had I been a parent, I wouldn't want my child to work with a suspected murderer. Except that I wasn't.

"I see. What does adjudication mean in this context? When I'm cleared of any involvement? When I'm acquitted? And who's making the decision that I'm cleared to be around?" I couldn't help but be a bit angry. I'd worked hard for Better Off Baking. These kids deserved the opportunity Layers would provide. I guess he felt I was taking it out on him.

He took a step backward. "Please, it's not my decision. The board and the superintendent made the choice. I'm just the messenger."

I understood, really. Embarrassed that I'd snapped at him, I went to the case. "Mister Rogers, I apologize for being rude. Can I make it up to you with a pastry?"

"No, but thank you. I'll be on my way now. How you want to handle the notifications to the interns is your choice."

The door closed behind him, the bell tinkling after his departure. I locked the door again, took a deep breath, and went into the kitchen.

The room was almost empty. Marie and Charlie had cleaned up, and Libby was gone. I expected her back for a two-thirty interview with Austin. I'd tell her separately. But I sat down across from Austin, who was mopping hot sauce off his chin and turning a page of my yearbook. Red smudges coated the bottom of the page.

"Austin, I have some bad news."

He looked up, and I looked into his blue eyes. I wondered what he considered bad news. "The county school district has suspended the Better Off Baking program indefinitely." He didn't need to know the details. But I'd be honest with his parents and Emily, of course. They deserved it.

Libby blew through the back door with an armful of mail which she dumped on the worktable. "I went to the post office to get the bakery mail. We got a ton to go through."

"Austin, if you would keep looking, I'd appreciate it. This isn't tied to the internship."

He shrugged and turned a page. I gathered up his trash and tossed it in the garbage. "So, no interview?"

"No, not today." I didn't know when. My heart began to ache. Isn't that what happens when dreams are shattered?

Chapter Twenty-Five

Libby's face reddened. "How come no interview?"

I scooped up the mail. "Let's go up to the office."

My head baker wasn't known for her patience. She followed me like a terrier, yipping at my heels over what was going on around here. The only respite was when she leaned over to scratch Rusty's tummy.

I made her sit across from me as she had this morning and dumped the pile of mail on the desk. The news I was to deliver wouldn't be welcome, and I hoped her reaction would be more subdued.

"Libby, the county schools have suspended our program until I am exonerated from any involvement in Reginald's murder."

She dropped her arms on top of the mail pile and bowed her head. Her posture said she was spent. There were no tears, only silence.

Then, after a minute, she straightened with a smirk on her face. "What will it take for your exoneration?" Her fingers curled the air around the word *exoneration*.

I sat back in the chair. "What comes to mind is when someone else is arrested."

Her eyes shined with the promise of a great idea. "What if you got a letter from the chief? I mean, saying you aren't involved in any way?" I know she was pondering asking Cameron to have his father write a letter. Frank Schwerin was still out of town.

"I don't think it would make a difference." I fingered the pile of mail in the middle of the desk. "We'll put the whole program on hold for the upcoming semester. We still have two more positions to fill, but I don't want to give anyone any false hope by doing interviews."

Her eyebrows drew together. "What's Austin doing then?"

"On Tuesday morning, he saw someone shooting out the camera at the Bishop Museum..."

Libby's eyes widened. "That's right across from Boulangerie." She was quick alright. "Maybe he was responsible..."

I cut her off. "The problem is, he doesn't know who it was."

Her enthusiasm deflated.

"I bribed him with lunch from Taco Bell if he'd go through my old high school yearbooks. Chances are the murderer is local. Maybe he'll find his picture. Then we'll have a name and can go to the police."

Another smirk. "Better not go to Foster. He's got it out for you."

I stifled a laugh. "I know." I rolled a hand over the pile of mail, ready to move on. "Let's go through this. It's been a week since I've picked it up."

Bills, receipts, and an order or two made up most of the stack. Sales notices, ads, and circulars were the balance, except for one letter, addressed to me in block printing that I didn't recognize.

Libby picked it up. "No return address. That's strange." She ripped the envelope open with a letter opener. Her face paled as she read the letter. She glanced at me and dropped it like it was on fire. "Sarah..."

I slid the paper across the desk and read.

> *"Stop asking questions that don't concern you, or you'll be sorry."*

Oh no. Who would send this?

The murderer, of course.

The young police officer who responded for the threats report wasn't impressed with the message. I'm sure it comes from seeing too much of what ugliness life has to offer. He was professional and courteous, but in his eyes, I saw he'd rather be on his coffee break. He took the letter, bagged it and the envelope, even though Libby and I had touched it. He said if any usable fingerprints turned up, he'd call and arrange for elimination prints.

Mine would be on file with the state for licensing as a certified shorthand reporter, but I didn't bother telling him.

Chapter Twenty-Six

The next morning, after little sleep, I woke up and made a batch of Mom's cucumber chips for dinner tonight at Wesley's. These cucumber slices would marinate in the refrigerator during the day, and I wouldn't have to put a salad together when I'd rather be visiting.

At Layers, I worked the front counter. The letter bothered me more than I could admit. But I refused to be cowered when so much was at stake. Better Off Baking was a terrific program with little overhead and lots of potential to salvage damaged kids. I'd be careful, subtle about my questions. Jake had a good idea, but I couldn't ask anyone to follow me around on the off chance that I'd find someone who had relevant information.

The morning rush was over, and Tiffani had gone on a break. I looked in on Austin, who had just arrived. He munched on a glazed, old-fashioned donut and leafed through the pages. I slapped a napkin on the table, but he didn't even look up.

I was tidying up the coffee bar when the doorbell chimed. A heavyset woman on the backside of forty strolled in. She slipped her purse over her shoulder to secure it as she leaned over to inspect the baked goods. Her eyes were alight with the bakery's delights.

I greeted her with a helpful, "Good morning. How can I help you today?"

"Oh, it all looks so good." She breathed in with the gasp of a sugar addict.

"Are you here for anything special, or are you looking around?"

"Um, I thought I'd take a coffee cake or some other pastries to my neighbor. She's lost her husband, you know, and I'd like to give her a coffee cake or a pastry to offer people who stop by."

I caught my breath. Then, took a chance that Judith Bateau was the only recently widowed neighbor in my small town.

"Judith Bateau?"

Fluffy, bleached blond hair waved up and down in a distracted acknowledgment.

"I heard about Reginald. You have my sympathies. I was acquainted with him..."

The woman cocked her head sideways. "No sympathies needed here. Reginald was a jerk. Judith will be much happier without him. We heard them arguing all the time. He was so mean to her." She leaned into the counter, pointing down at the white chip and macadamia nut coffee cake. "Does that have nuts in it?"

"Yes, it does. Are you allergic?"

"No, I don't care for them. Raisins are my favorite."

"Well, then." I had a thought. "If this is for Judith and you might like a piece, I've got just the answer. But you will have to wait a little."

"Yes?" Her pudgy face positively glowed with sugar lust.

"I have a cinnamon coffee cake ready to come out of the oven in twenty minutes."

"Ohhh, marvelous." She glanced at her watch. "Darn, I have an errand to run. But I'll be back to pick it up in an hour. Hope it'll still be warm."

"I have a better idea. I'll deliver it as soon as it comes out of the oven, and you can enjoy a piece with Judith when you're done."

"You'd do that? Marvelous."

"Here's a card for you to fill out so Judith knows it's from you."

She scribbled happily; a quick scowl evaporated as she looked askance at the coffee cakes.

"Now, I just need the address."

Refrigerated Cucumber Chips

- *1 or 2 cucumbers, depending on size*
- *¼ cup sugar*
- *¾ cup cider vinegar*
- *¾ cups water*
- *½ tsp. salt*
- *½ tsp. mustard seed*
- *Pinch of black pepper*

Peel cucumbers. Score sides lengthwise with a fork. Cut into ¼ inch slices. Mix remaining ingredients, add cucumbers, and refrigerate for 2-4 hours. Enjoy soon—they get soggy after day two.

Chapter Twenty-Seven

"I got him. Here he is!" Austin's shout filled the kitchen.

I rushed to Austin's table from the front. Thankfully, there were no customers at the moment. He had my freshman yearbook open to the senior portraits. Beside the portraits was a collage of candid shots from basketball games. The photo of Mark Gibson in a tux sat beside an action shot of two players at a Bishop Broncos junior varsity basketball tournament game.

Austin stabbed at the photo. "This is him. It's him."

I studied the pictures. Austin's finger smudged both the portrait of Mark and the action shot beside him of a basketball player slam dunking a ball. Dread made a fist in my stomach. Another question raised about Mark. But I had to be sure. "Austin. Which one of these two men did you see?"

His face flushed. "They're two different guys?"

My heart sunk. So much for an identification.

"Yes."

"They look so much alike, except for the nose. And

you really can't see that in this picture. He's facing straight on." His eyes were like saucers. "I'm sorry. I thought I could help."

I put a hand on his shoulder. "Thanks for all the time you spent on this, Austin. I appreciate your diligence."

He stood, crumbs cascading from his shirt. "I'm sorry."

But he did help. He narrowed the field down to two. But I didn't like the results. Mark Gibson, who I hated to think could've done such a heinous act, and the basketball player, Ed Strange, who had no known motive. Ed wasn't on anyone's radar as a suspect.

As I boxed up the warm coffee cake, I decided I'd keep the results of Austin's search to myself. I saw no benefit in muddying the waters with this information. Nor did I want any more pressure on the Gibsons. They'd be home in a few days, and I dreaded the thought of them seeing Mark behind bars.

Chapter Twenty-Eight

Twenty minutes later, I rang the doorbell at 1589 Bear Creek Drive. Judith answered without a smile.

"I have a delivery from a caring neighbor. The card is on top."

A glint of recognition sparked in her eyes, and she waved me inside, arm bracelets and bangles clicking as she pointed to the left into the kitchen.

Judith snatched the card, tore open the envelope, and after reading it, tossed it on a butcherblock counter. "She's not concerned. She's nosy and wants me to invite her to share the cake."

Reginald and Judith shared their uncharitable view of people. I was mildly surprised to see her face made up perfectly. No red eyes, no tissues lying around. One would hardly surmise this was a house of mourning by the evidence.

"I'm sure she wanted to be kind in this time of your distress."

She snorted, and her pinched face looked more

annoyed than mournful. "People are out for their own gain. She's no exception."

"I'm sure she wanted to comfort you. Your loss must be..."

"...must be none of your business, Sarah Murray." She sniffed, turning away.

Here I was affirming her most recent observation on humanity. "Judith, I'll be honest. I worked with Reginald several months ago. Now, he wasn't the easiest person to deal with, but I'm looking for people who might wish him ill. The police haven't come up with any suspects yet. I think the job can be done better."

She poked an index finger at her chin. Like she'd changed her mind about me, she said, "At least you're honest, Sarah." She sighed. "I've got people making offers on the business, the building, and this house. Acting all coy, but after what I have. I haven't even decided what to do with it all. The cops won't let me in to clean the place up yet, so I can't sell it right now. It's a real mess inside." She took a breath as if getting all this off her chest was doing her good. She seemed to be thinking out loud. "And I'm not moving from here. Yet. Depends on the state of our finances."

I waited while she thought. "That darn banker has been after me for a meeting. I know he was pressuring Reginald, but I don't know for what. He wasn't too smart with his money, you know. Reginald, I mean." Making the clarification, she smiled to herself.

The banker. "Which banker, Judith?" I thought I recalled the bank where we made deposits during my brief time as a manager two months ago. But I wasn't sure, and Reginald was so erratic, he could've changed banks.

"Whatshisname from the Owens Valley Bank."

"Could it be Larry Nixon?" Nixon was the loan officer who was handling the improvement loan for Layers' front room. It would be incredible luck if he was also Reginald's banker.

"Nixon?" Her face was a mask of a quizzical stare. "Oh yes. Nixon? No, Nixon, that's right." She shook her head, clearing it of such unimportant matters. "Reginald did the finances both for the business and the family. His mother left him the bakery, you know. He said it was keeping afloat but not much more than that. He told me to cut my household spending. With all the traveling he's been doing? And business, my eye. He had something else going." With an indignant huff, she said, "Cut my spending? Can you imagine? We were bare bones as it was. And he told me to stop paying Ed for mowing the lawn. It's a good retirement job for my brother. God knows that Reg never mowed the lawn."

"My gosh. It's a miracle you endured." I hated pandering to this self-centered, vindictive woman.

"Oh, that reminds me." She turned to face me. She'd been in some dark place and had now returned, her eyes sharp and piercing. "I have two loads of flour, sugar, and such that were delivered in the back parking lot at Boulangerie this morning. With our manager gone, I didn't know there was a delivery coming. We can't use the shipment, and much of the stuff has an expiration date, so I'll sell it to you—at a discount."

I scrambled, reviewing what I could of Libby's orders and trying to figure whether she could cancel Layers's next delivery. I decided to take a chance. Boulangerie's load would fill our needs for the month. We haggled over a price for a moment—it was clear Judith had no idea how much the shipment would cost to other wholesale buyers. I offered a reasonable amount, and we agreed on a deal.

I heard the front door fly open. Ed Strange marched into the kitchen and stood before us, red-faced, fists clenched then unclenching. "What do you think you're doing here?" He spat as he spoke. "Rubbing our noses in our misfortune?"

"No, Ed. I…"

"You are responsible for all this."

"I was leaving." I ignored his posturing, which seemed to inflame him more.

He sputtered, "Leave her alone. She's in mourning, for God's sake."

"Judith, I'll be in touch to pay you for the supplies." I left before Ed could think of any more insults.

Chapter Twenty-Nine

I hurried down the path to my car. At the curb, a green '70s model pickup truck pulled up, and Devon Bateau spilled out. The truck sat running, its driver watching and listening with the passenger door open. Judging by the glassy-eyed glare I got from Devon, he'd had some alcoholic solace. He wobbled his way to me. "You're a nervy one, aren't you?"

"Devon, whatever you've heard about me being responsible for your father's…"

"Save it." He raised his hand to stop me. "I don't care. Dad wasn't exactly a model father." He shook his head. "He spent more time with his basset hound than he did with me." He burped. "Good riddance to bad rubbish."

"Devon, he was your father…"

"He wasn't a father. He was a cardboard cutout of what a father should be. He didn't care about me. He cared about what the community thought about him."

The truck driver hollered. "Yeah, like Mister Evers."

Devon grunted with a memory. "I'm going to be a

senior this year. Dad wanted me to go to college." His eyes blazed with fury. "I never wanted to go to college. My counselor, Mister Evers, gets me, you know?"

"It's good to have a counselor who knows you and your preferences."

"Last semester, Mister Evers started looking around for vocational schools for mechanics. That's what I wanna do. But when Dad found out, he hit the ceiling. He went down and yelled at my counselor."

"This happened in the spring?"

"Yeah, but now school's starting up in a few weeks, and Dad went on the offensive again." Devon hiccuped. "He's been calling Mister Evers, bugging him to talk me into going to a university."

The young man lost his balance while standing. I grabbed him and looped my arm around his elbow. In a voice that wouldn't allow for disagreement, I said, "Follow me." I marched him up the sidewalk to the front door, where I rang the doorbell. Ed opened the door. Before he could say a word, I gently pushed Devon inside. Ed wrapped an arm around his nephew. "Honestly, Devon. I came all the way up from Big Pine and find you like this."

I left while Ed Strange was busy.

The driver of the red truck waited at the curb. I took it as a sign that he wanted to talk to me, so I closed the passenger-side door and walked to the driver's side. The engine heat and the midday sun combined to a scorching temperature as I stood near the driver.

"Did you hear what he said?" I asked the pimple-faced teen boy.

"Yeah. His dad was a real…"

I held my hand up to stop him. "Think of a word you can use in church to describe him."

The kid grinned in embarrassment. "He was like a demon. Yeah, that fits. He'd get all physical, yelling and screaming. It was like he was possessed." His eyes searched mine, like so many people do—to be sure he was heard. He was.

"That fits with what I've seen too. What about the counselor?"

"Mister Evers?" The kid shrugged. "He's a good guy, all right. He didn't deserve the ration that Mister Bateau gave him."

"Ration?"

"Yeah, I saw him on campus one day last spring. He followed Mister Evers to his car, yelling at him the whole way."

"What did Mister Evers do?"

The kid cocked his head. "You know, he was kind of classy. He ignored Dev's Dad; he kept right on walking."

I patted the top of the truck door near the kid's suntanned arm. "Thanks for your insight. I appreciate it." I wondered if there was a motive for murder in the badgering of Mister Evers.

As the truck zoomed off, I checked my phone for the time. Almost one o'clock. It was still summer, but teachers were often at school off-term.

I'd take a chance.

Chapter Thirty

The campus of Bishop Union High School is shaded by generations-old sycamore, elm, and locust trees. Built in 1922, the stucco façade stands a three-story building with a capacity of seven hundred students. But today, there were few people on the grounds. At the office, I found the counseling offices within the guidance wing on the near side of the parking lot. The office clerk had no idea if Harlan Evers was in his office or not. I went to see.

The door was propped open, and I entered. A tall, slender man with short, cropped, light-brown hair stood at a desk arranging binders.

"Mister Evers?"

He looked up. Bright blue eyes with a sharp intelligence met my gaze. A tentative smile touched his thin lips as if he wasn't sure if I was a friend or foe. "Yes."

"I'm Sarah Murray. I'm an acquaintance of Devon Bateau."

Evers's spine straightened, ready for an assault.

"Yes." he said again, with a finality that told me I wouldn't get much information from him.

"I'm here because he told me that you and his father, Reginald, had a difference of opinion about Devon's future." When on a fishing expedition, use the simplest bait.

His eyes narrowed. "That's no secret."

"So he said. His friend said Mister Bateau followed you to your car, yelling at you all the way. Badgering was the word he used."

"Then you have a witness." He shoved a binder sideways. "Does this have anything to do with his murder?"

"I'm not sure." I tried to get back on track. "What was he yelling about? Was it over Devon's desire to go to vocational school instead of college?"

"It's not uncommon these days. Universities are expensive, and kids don't want to drag around student loans for the rest of their lives." He shrugged. "Vocational schools offer better opportunities for some kids. Devon wants to be a mechanic. A degree in engineering isn't going to get him a job at a dealership."

"True. I'm a believer. I'm most interested in how Mister Bateau thought he could coerce you to convince Devon."

"I guess he thought I wielded some serious influence on the boy. That's not true. I had some information sent to the boy, and his dad found it. Mister Bateau flipped his lid."

I suspected that Reginald had some power over this counselor. A little bit of backyard blackmail? But I had to use the right words to get through to him. "Did Mister Bateau use some kind of leverage on you to come to his side?"

"I couldn't comment on that." Evers looped his arms

across his chest. "Now, if you'll excuse me, I have work to do."

"Was Reginald Bateau angry with you about his son's future?"

"Who are you? Why do you want to know?"

I stretched the truth a bit. "I'm a friend of the family trying to get to the bottom of this disagreement." It was clear my special wording had failed. But I had to find out what I could.

"I have nothing more to say to you."

"I'll leave after one last question. Since you're not in school now, your days are free, right?"

"If you call this free." He waved at the piles of paper and binders.

"Tuesday morning, did you stop at a bakery for coffee and a pastry?"

He took a step around the desk toward me. "If I did, I wouldn't tell you. Now leave."

I wasn't afraid. He didn't have that kind of menace that put me in jeopardy. But this man's evasions were as off as sour milk.

I left anyway.

Chapter Thirty-One

I'd made a coffee date with Emily for today at two o'clock. I'd finished with Harlan Evers sooner than I planned, so I drove into the parking lot at Wye Road Feeds early by a half hour.

From the doorway, Emily waved me in. The store was quiet except for the hum of a tractor working in the backyard. She steered me to the coffee room behind the counter and plopped in a seat across from me.

"Coffee?"

"Thanks, I'll pass. Maybe a glass of water."

"That sounds good to me too." She went to the freezer/refrigerator and put our drinks together. Her sweet smile made me happy as she handed me a plastic cup with ice water in it. "I know you tried to get Austin into the program."

Her expression said she knew he had failed. "Now, wait a minute. I set up an interview that we had to cancel for now."

Her blue eyes looked mournful. "Austin told me what happened with county schools. It's a darn shame, I say."

"Yes, it is. But whenever Reginald Bateau's murderer is caught, I'll be in the clear. Then they'll open the program back up."

"You think you can wait that long? The police here aren't known for their speedy work."

I shrugged. "I'm asking my own questions. Maybe I can hurry up the solution."

"What about Mark Gibson? Wouldn't he want Reginald to find justice? After all, Reg was the guy who knocked Melody down, making her a target for her real murderer."

"No, I don't think so. Mark arrived in town…"

Then, I realized it. "Emily, I don't know when he arrived, only when he showed up at Layers. I left when Javier called, but I didn't really believe Mark would've had time to get to Boulangerie and kill Reginald before I arrived. Even though twenty minutes passed between Javier's call and my arrival… I am sure that would be enough time to murder Reginald."

Emily sat back, blown away by the possibility of Mark's culpability. "What are you going to do, Sarah?"

I waved the thought away. "I'm not sure Mark knew Reginald's part in the whole incident."

"Are you going to the police?"

"No. They don't need some ambiguous news like this. None of this means anything. And passing on this information to the cops would look like I'm spreading the blame to avoid my own guilt."

"Do you have any idea what is going on in the investigation?"

"I have no idea." I sat back in the chair, a hundred ideas pelting my brain at the same time.

"Doesn't that cop guy you're seeing clue you in?"

I shook my head. "They wouldn't tell him. He's in a different jurisdiction a long way from here."

Emily looked dismayed. "Not too far, I hope."

"Seven to eight hours on a good day. He's up in Northern California, Petaluma."

Her nose crinkled at the distance. "Too bad." The chimes announcing a customer rang. Emily shook her head. "Don't worry, Nancy will get it. Now, go on. What's your next move?"

"I've made an appointment with the banker, Larry Nixon. He's handling the loan on Layers, and I'll be checking up on that. But he's also Reginald Bateau's banker. I want to see what I can find out about Bateau's finances. Maybe he has some information that could shed some light on the murder."

Chapter Thirty-Two

After a quick run back to Layers to let Rusty out for a break, I drove into the parking lot of the Owens Valley Bank at five minutes to three. The afternoon hadn't gotten as hot as the weather reporter had said, and I'd enjoyed my time outside with my dog. I was looking forward to the afternoon walks again when fall settled in. Another month of hot weather was predicted to wane. The next few weeks would tell how long fall would be. Even downtown, I could tell the rabbitbrush was blooming. The smell was like an old, wet tennis shoe, but after being gone for ten years, the smell was welcome, even if it produced a few sneezes.

The blast of air conditioning hit me when I entered the bank. A glance around showed me to Larry Nixon's office. The door was open, and Larry was seated at his desk. The office was a sterile bank space with a department store painting on one wall and bookshelves on the other. The focus of the room was a wall of glass overlooking Main Street, darkened with cling film to obscure the view into the room.

I announced myself, and he stood, reaching across his desk to shake hands.

We both sat in our respective chairs, and he leaned into his clasped hands that he'd placed on the desk. "You're here about your expansion loan for Layers Bakery?"

"Yes." I folded my hands in my lap, feeling a bit like I was at the principal's office for some unforeseen trouble I'd caused. I felt guilty. That was it. I didn't like lying and manipulating people to get the answers I needed. But there was no other way. No arrests have been made. My friend and Inyo County Deputy, Kelly McSorley, was my pipeline into local law enforcement, and he would've told me if BPD had any solid leads on a suspect. I hadn't heard from him.

"I know all I can do is wait for the loan committee's approval next week, but I have a hypothetical question."

"Hypothetical? I don't usually get those kinds of questions." He smiled, barely concealing his trepidation.

"This is hypothetical, mind you. I just spoke to Judith Bateau." I paused for emphasis, then noted the slight tic under his left eye. "Say, hypothetically, that Boulangerie banks here. Judith is indicating she may sell the bakery. I got the impression she may come to me first to make an offer." This was a gross exaggeration of our conversation, if not an outright lie.

His brows shot up. "Oh?"

"I might be interested in the purchase, but in light of the loan request I have being processed with you, I wonder if expanding Layers might be delayed." I was going to hell. There was no way I could afford to buy Boulangerie.

He chewed on my words for a moment. "And you

think you might want to put the loan process on hold for now?"

"Here's the problem—it's too early to encourage Judith to make any decisions. Reginald's funeral is tomorrow, and she's still grieving."

"Yes, a terrible affair, his murder." He shook his head in disbelief that such an incident could happen in Bishop. The illusion of small-town safety had been shattered, leaving its grim reality hanging over the entire community.

"Unless," I drew out the syllables until I was sure I had all of his attention. "Unless there is something in Boulangerie's accounts that would necessitate a speedy transaction." I was going to hell, for sure. "Something to benefit Judith and the bank."

I let the thought percolate.

Finally, he cleared his throat. "You know, of course, that I cannot divulge any account information for Boulangerie or the Bateau family."

"Of course." I waited.

"However, if I was you, I'd pull the expansion loan for now." He sat back in his plush upholstered chair, fidgeting. He'd given up information that should have been private.

Now I knew two things: first, Boulangerie and probably the Bateau family were in need of financial rescue. Second, it would be months before I see any café expansion money. But how did the first point get me closer to the murderer?

"Then, I'd like to stop the extension loan." I rubbed my eyes, faking a moment of dilemma. "The café can wait. But now I have a bigger issue. Would this bank be a good fit for a commercial loan to purchase Boulangerie?" I know I sounded coy, but I had to know more.

"Why, yes. We'll be happy to look at your loan request—once it comes through."

I sighed, hoping to sound pleased with his response. "I worked with Reginald some months ago to try and get Boulangerie back on track financially. We did, but he remained unpredictable and temperamental, to say the least. His outbursts were the reason the employees walked out the first time. Our association ended when it became apparent that he resented any camaraderie I had developed with the staff. The day he was murdered, his store manager called me to say Reginald was having a temper tantrum. He fired all his employees, and during the manager's call, I heard him yelling and throwing stuff around. But I'd seen it before."

Larry Nixon's tic practically vibrated off his face.

"Mister Nixon, did you ever experience anything like that from him?"

He began to nod, then stopped and coughed. "He wasn't always easy to be around. Especially when he wasn't getting his way."

"I also know that he played people like chess pieces." *Look who's talking.* "He had an issue with one of his son's counselors at the high school. I believe he was exerting pressure on the counselor to get his way."

Nixon's eyebrows shot up again. My comment had hit home. "Maybe not blackmail or anything as serious as that, but he had *leverage*. You know what I mean?"

He rubbed his damp palms together and stood. "Thank you for coming in, Sarah. You let me know when or if I can be of financial assistance." The way he'd stressed financial cemented my belief that Reginald had some kind of power over him too.

Okay, why was the bank pressuring Reginald when he

was the one who was blackmailing the banker? Maybe Judith had it wrong. Maybe the bank wasn't going at Reginald, but the other way around?

Chapter Thirty-Three

Almost four o'clock. Rusty must be in misery. I had to go back to Layers and pick him up. It was only six blocks from the bank to the bakery. I parked in the Layers employee lot behind the bakery.

The shop was all closed up, but Libby's motorbike was on the walk at the back door. I let myself in and called for Rusty. As he sprinted downstairs, I caught sight of Libby. Leaning on the worktable, perched on a stool, she held her head in her hands.

Trouble. "Libby, I'll be right back. I have to let Rusty out."

She flicked her hand in acknowledgment.

We were back in less than five minutes. With Rusty at my feet, I slid onto a stool next to Libby. "What's going on, Lib?"

She hadn't been crying, but her eyes held the weight of her father's sins. "The house sold. By this time next week, you'll have new neighbors. It's closing escrow in record time, they say."

I put a hand on her shoulder for comfort. She seemed

to draw reassurance from my touch. This was the close of an ugly chapter of her life. "It's good to move on, Libby. Now you must."

"I'm tired of being in a holding pattern. I want to move on. Couch surfing is overrated. I want a place of my own. I'm looking at an apartment this afternoon at five. A place on West Elm." Her gaze searched my face, I suspected she was looking for approval.

"Nice neighborhood, sweetie. This is a positive change for you."

"I guess." She traced imaginary lines on the aluminum surface of the worktable. "I still have to decide about my father."

"Decide what?" I wondered when this would come up.

Her sigh came up from her toes. "Whether I forgive him or not. I don't know if I can stand by him during the court proceedings, then jail." No, honey, I wanted to say. Jail is for short sentences; prison is where he's going. It's for long sentences, like life. But she didn't need to hear it now.

"Maybe you can take your time making this decision. Is there any reason you need to make it now?"

"I meet with him on Monday. He's the legal owner of the home, and he's going to sign a quitclaim deed to put it in my name. We have to do that so I can sell it. His legal fees are coming out of the proceeds."

As a court reporter, I'd seen some victims speak in court about the trauma the defendant had caused. It was a painful, grueling process that required courage and conviction. A consequence was that, for some, it afforded the only opportunity to speak to the person responsible. The program touted that it 'offered closure' to victims. I was skeptical that most of the victims ever learned to come to terms with their trauma and pain. I saw it first-hand in my friend and thought Libby would live with this for the rest of her life. "You've done the really tough task —facing him, telling him how much he hurt you. But don't let his sins confuse you with evil."

"Huh?"

"Your father isn't evil. He did some good things, like marrying your mom, having and raising you. What he did was wrong, clearly. He was influenced by evil. Evil is all around us, all the time. You have to fight it off every day. You are a terrific example of battling evil, right?"

"You mean, like, skipping school and partying?"

"Exactly. You made choices that steered you on the right path, away from that stuff. He didn't."

"Okay, I get that. And, you're right. Being where I am in life, here—" She waved her arm to encompass all of Layers. "—with Melody, and you, have made me stronger." She sat up straight. "I know I can cope with this. It's forgiving him that I don't think I can do."

"Forgiveness and judgment are different matters. What Grant did was wrong, and he will be judged."

"You mean...?" She pointed a solemn index finger upward.

I smiled and nodded, with a wish that the answers were as simple as I'd presented them. "God has forgiven him. Now, it's up to you to do the same—when you can. Your father will need that to make amends. He'll have the rest of his life to atone."

She sat quietly, contemplating.

I had a thought. "Maybe you can get his attorney to get the signature?"

"I'll call him and ask."

"It won't hurt."

"I hate seeing him." Her face screwed up in a

grotesque mask. "I never liked my father. Isn't that an awful thing to say? I'm not sure I'll ever forgive him."

"You can forgive when your heart is in it. Forgiveness will take time. Don't rush it." I exhaled, tired suddenly. "As for the house, the sooner you get that behind you, the better."

A tentative smile broke through her long face. "You always have the right words to say to me. Just like Melody did."

Her hand reached out and covered mine. "What would I do without you?"

I sniffed. "Ah, you'd be fine. You need to trust yourself. You've had some hard knocks in your life, but none were your doing. You have sound instincts, Libby. Trust them."

"I've got some strong people in my life. They help too." She leaned an elbow on the worktable and propped her head on a hand. "You, Cameron, my friend Yesenia who lets me bunk with her…"

"How is Cameron? I haven't heard much about him lately."

"He's out woodin' with his dad. Their permit is for Deadman Summit area. They should fill his truck with firewood." Her eyes lit up, and she grabbed my arm. "Oh, wait. Before he left, he said his dad was thawing toward me." She gazed at the kitchen—her kitchen, now. "I guess he can see how hard I work. That seems to make a difference to him."

"It does to most people our age." Cameron's dad had a good decade on me—in his mid to late forties—but anyone over Libby's age would be all lumped together and considered ancient.

"Whatever the reason, I'm glad he's not causing you any trouble."

Rusty snorted. His feet paddled in his sleep. I pictured his doggie dream of running through a meadow, chasing a ball.

A glance at the clock told me it was time for us both to leave. "You should get moving if you're going to make that appointment to see that apartment."

"Right." She slid her small frame off the stool and tucked it under the table. With this small action, she showed me how much she'd grown in the past few months. Her tidiness and responsibility were apparent but not boastful. I was proud of her. I hoped that soon Better Off Baking could help more kids like her. At the back door, she stopped. "Oh, by the way, Austin said he'd be back tomorrow."

I nodded a thanks as she put-putted off on her motorbike. I ran to Tom and Anna's to feed the kitties. Then, to McLaren House to pick up my contribution to the meal and off to dinner at Wesley's.

Chapter Thirty-Four

Dinner was at Wesley's. Melody's two kitties were safely ensconced in the safety of a tree, while they squinted at Arco and Rusty romping in the front yard in the shade of the elms. Wesley made a nice dinner for a real family get-together. He'd made up a pasta and andouille sausage dish that would go well with the cucumber chips I'd made earlier this morning. From the bakery, I'd brought a pan of Charlie's cornbread and an eight-inch pecan pie using a new recipe Marie had found.

The wooden picnic table in the sideyard was set for three, Wesley, Jake, and me. The scrub-filled hillocks sprouted between gulches where rain coursed from the adjacent Sierra Mountains during the sparse storms. The high desert lay mere steps away from the Charters' house. The nearest neighbor was at Keough's Hot Springs, three miles away.

Months ago, some of Wesley's congregation had put a white cross and silk flowers on the site of Melody's assault. At thirty feet from the road that dead-ended at Wesley's driveway, it was visible from the house. Mel had been a vibrant and meaningful part of the Bishop community, and her loss was felt by many. Their well-meaning memorial dredged up memories Wesley was having difficulty working through. Thankfully, Wesley's neighbors quietly removed the memorial so he wouldn't be reminded every moment he looked over the desert landscape.

"Nico, my neighbor down the street, took down all the memorial materials from Mel's... from where she fell. He did it yesterday."

"It must be a relief not to have to see it whenever you look out the window."

He nodded, dishing the cucumber chips into a bowl.

"Where's Mark?" I asked as I sat, savoring the cooling breeze.

Wesley gave a one-shoulder shrug as he put the bowl of pasta in the middle of the table. He didn't care enough to give his shrug both shoulders. "Dunno. He comes and goes as he wishes."

Jake's eyes twinkled. "You're not your brother's keeper?"

Wesley smirked as he sat down across from me. I dished the cucumbers into the three bowls and distributed them. The men heaped pasta and sausages on their plates and dug in.

Jake wouldn't let it go. "It's amazing he has so many friends here to visit."

Wesley unconsciously shoved the marinara-covered rotini around his plate. He didn't like what he had to say. "He's not visiting. He's passing time, waiting for Tom and Anna to get back. I think he's got something planned for them." He buttered the cornbread with a ferocity it didn't deserve.

"It sounds like you think it's something Tom and

Anna won't appreciate."

"You know Mark…"

Jake, to his credit, kept quiet. He didn't know Mark, really.

But I did. "Do you think there's anything we can do to protect them from him?"

"He's their son. They may want to see him. It's been eleven years since he left, and now, they don't have Melody. He's their only child."

"But you don't believe that do you?" I knew he didn't.

Jake asked, "Any idea what he may have planned?" From the narrowing of his eyes, I saw Jake was in protection mode. A memory flashed as I saw Dad watching videos of old movies—Hopalong Cassidy on a white horse chasing a bad guy, heading the black hat off at the pass. I'd grown up with stories about the Westerns that were part of our local history. Hundreds of films from the '20s to the '50s were filmed in Lone Pine, the Alabama Hills, less than an hour from here. They were part of the local fabric of the community, that white-hatted cowboy persona. Jake was a white-hatted hero.

"Not a clue, but I suspect it'll have something to do with Melody." It dawned on me that Mark's efforts might also be directed at Wesley, maybe me too. Anyone who loved his sister.

It was my turn to feel the protectiveness. I'd loved Melody and Wesley together. Now I was finding Wesley was even more precious than I'd known before. With her good sense, Melody had fallen in love and chosen to spend her short life with him. He was a good man. He had—and was still—suffering at the loss of his wife. I wondered at the damage Mark could do.

Sensing his discomfort on the topic of his brother-in-law, I changed the subject. "Did Sergeant Foster interview you?" I sliced the pecan pie and laid out three generous slices.

"Yeah, and I had an alibi that was easy. I was sitting in the offices of the Owens Valley Bank at that time, so I'm on camera with witnesses."

Jake didn't get the memo about changing the subject. "Talking about alibis, did anyone check into Mark's? I mean, the fact that he showed up that morning at your bakery, then had twenty minutes to kill Reginald shouldn't be ignored."

"That's the kind of garbage I'd expect from a cop." Mark's strident voice cut across the conversation as he walked up to the table, rumpled and sweaty.

Jake looked at Mark without flinching. I saw the debate in Jake—stand to fight or sit and let it pass. He sat. For now.

"I can't believe it. It's like no time has passed. You're still all against me." Mark slurred his words. His eyes were bloodshot, and bits of white spit formed at the corner of his lips.

"Now, Mark." Wesley began with an appeasing tone.

"Don't you 'now Mark' me, you holier than thou preacher man." Mark glared at Wesley, then wiped his brow with his shirt tail, showing an almost emaciated midriff. "You never liked me. You tried to poison Melody against me. I haven't done nothin'. I came back to make peace, and here you are spreading lies about me."

"Well, what about it?" Jake stood, squaring with Mark. "Where did you go after your visit to see Sarah?"

"You're getting nothin' from me. You're not a cop here." Mark stumbled and caught himself on the corner of a bare flower box. He glowered at me. I'm sure he believed that I told the cops about his arrival. I decided against trying to defend myself. Mark was drunk and, even if he'd been sober, wouldn't likely have listened to me.

Jake moved away from the table and took a step toward Mark. He reached out to steady him, but Mark slapped his hand away.

"Get away from me..." Mark muttered. He twisted away from Jake and the table, weaving to the house.

"Mark, so you know," Jake caught Mark's attention. He paused at the doorway but didn't turn to Jake. "Sarah didn't tell the cops about your return."

Mark swayed when he glanced at me, then licked his lips. Without saying a word, he turned, pushed the screen door open, and let it slam shut.

Wesley ran a hand over his forehead, beginning an apology. Jake stopped him and sat down. "He's not yours to be sorry about, Wes. Don't worry about it."

But I did. I'm sure Jake did too. What did Mark do between the time I threw him out of Layers and the time I found Reginald dead?

Pecan Pie

- *1 cup white corn syrup*
- *1 cup dark corn syrup*
- *4 eggs*
- *½ cup sugar*
- *½ cup flour*
- *1 tbs. vanilla*
- *2 cups lightly toasted chopped pecans*

Beat eggs and sugar. Add flour and beat through. Add corn syrups, vanilla, and—lastly—pecans. Pour into an unbaked 8-inch pie shell. Bake for 45 minutes at 375 degrees. Cool for at least 3 hours before cutting.

Chapter Thirty-Five

I was feeling more than ever like I'd hit a brick wall after Mark's scene last night. Jake had been called back to work for an emergency and left early this morning. He said he'd be back sometime next week. I sighed my frustration, thinking hard about where to go next. The answer was easy, although not the one I was looking for—time to go to work.

After the bakery closed at two o'clock, I'd sneak into the funeral home where Reginald's services were being held. As much as I disliked the man, he deserved my final respects. I hoped to get in and out without the family seeing me.

Saturday was my normal day off, but Anna was still out, due to return home this morning. We opened later than weekdays because the foot traffic didn't support opening at six-thirty. By ten o'clock, our coffee cakes for weekenders had come and gone. I wiped down the display case with smeared preschoolers' fingerprints when I heard the bell tinkle.

"Javier." I greeted the newcomer.

"Miss Sarah." He nodded with respect and pulled off his ball cap. Holding it in both hands, he walked across the open space that I hoped would someday be a café.

"It's good to see you, Javier," I said as we shook hands. "You want some coffee? A pastry?"

He held up a hand. "No, thank you. I came to ask if you need any help." He couldn't help an appreciative glance at the display cabinet.

"Are you planning on going back to work at Boulangerie?"

He tilted his head with skepticism. "No one knows when or if Miss Judith will open. But you are open now."

Wishing I had a table to sit at with him, I poured a cup of coffee. He declined, and I motioned him into the kitchen. Libby was hard at work, with only Marie assisting today. Charlie was off and would be in tomorrow.

With his help, I pulled a couple of stools out. I arranged them at the opposite end of Libby's work area and had him sit. All this time, I mulled over the next few months of Layers' future, as I hoped it would go. Had the expansion loan gone through, it would've meant construction, noise, and confusion for the next few weeks. That wouldn't happen, which looked like a blessing in disguise. That was one less issue for me to worry about.

"I've seen your work, Javier. I know what you can do." I sipped my coffee. He was a good baker, but his greatest skill was managing a kitchen well. We'd be lucky to have him. "Libby, can you take a break for a minute?"

Libby wiped the flour off her hands on her apron and came over. I introduced them, and they bumped fists. "Libby, how would you like some help? Now, but especially in the next two weeks when school begins."

She scrutinized him up and down. "Can you bake?"

"Yes, miss."

"He managed Boulangerie when I left. He'd been baking for…" I looked at him for an answer.

"Fourteen years, miss."

They chatted a few minutes, Libby asking about a flower nail, piping bag, and what number tip to use to make a rosette. She nodded, happy with his answers. Then, she pulled out a piping bag and asked him to decorate a small sheet of parchment paper. Javier painstakingly pressed all the designs Libby asked for. Beads of sweat shone on his forehead when he finally pushed the results back to her.

After a full inspection, Libby gave us both a thumbs up. She shouted, "Welcome!" and returned to rolling out sugar cookies.

"You've passed the interview. Libby is the only one you need to please. Now, I can't pay you the income that Boulangerie gave you, but I can put you to work. My own goal is to go back to work my own job in the new year. I need someone to replace me. It would be easier to leave knowing that Layers is in your and Libby's hands.

We settled on terms with a handshake. I sipped my cold coffee. "Did the police interview you about Reginald's rant?"

His dark eyes took on a mournful look. "Yes. He was very angry. He fired everybody."

"Did he say what he was upset about?"

Javier tipped his head while he thought. "He kept saying that we cost him too much money. He threw flour on the ground and said we were like that, wasted money."

I thought back on the weeks I'd helped him out last

spring. "But Javier, Boulangerie was bringing in money. We always had deposits for the bank—every day."

"Yes, I remember. But he took the books away from me when you left." Javier's eyes drooped with the insult he must have suffered.

"Where did that money go?" It was a rhetorical question. Javier wouldn't have any way of knowing. Would he? I recalled a criminal case I worked on last year. The defense proposed the assault defendant was a victim of a gambling addiction. Rather than a common pathology of alcohol abuse, the defendant had exhibited attention-seeking behaviors along with poor impulse control.

Reginald had always been a grandstander. He was the poster boy of Sunrise Club, a local nonprofit that raised money for schools. He was constantly in the *Inyo Register,* announcing some fundraising event or another. That was a flimsy indicator of a gambling addiction, but what else could wipe out Boulangerie profits so fast?

I shook my head at the mystery. "It's a sorry matter to lose your profitable business through reckless behavior."

"A very sad thing."

"Sad for a lot of people. Are you or any other employees going to the funeral?"

He shook his head. "I don't feel it's the right thing to do. He died after firing us all. Everyone else feels the same. No one is going."

I asked about the rest of the staff from Boulangerie, most of whom I'd gotten to know. He gave me the lowdown on the crew. Many had found jobs in local restaurants; some had moved from the area to places with a more lucrative job market.

I thought about Judith and Devon and the uncertainty they also faced. Especially his wife and son. "It's too bad he left his family behind with a difficult financial situation."

His lips pressed together in an odd expression, like he'd remembered something that was distressing. "He called his wife right before I called you. He was very mad. He yelled at her, called her bad names."

Puzzled, I considered what would make him so angry at his wife. Money and influence seemed to be the biggest reasons for his discontent, but Judith wouldn't have spent any bakery money.

What did Judith know that she wasn't telling?

Chapter Thirty-Six

J avier was happy to start immediately. After introducing him to Marie and showing him the cash register and espresso maker (to the best of my ability—I still had problems with that darn steamer), I went upstairs to gather the necessary paperwork.

Rusty's tail thumped against the landing floor, and I leaned over to scratch under his ear. I swear he smiled at me. I promised him a break while Javier filled out the application and government forms. Feeling lighter than I had in days, I trotted downstairs with papers attached to a clipboard and pen. Javier smiled as I handed them over.

My phone chimed a message.

From Mom: *We're home, tired and dirty, but safe.*

I texted back: *I'll be there soon.* I told Javier that I'd be back in a short while, to go to Libby for any problems, except for the espresso machine. He'd be on his own with that monster. She wasn't any better with it than me.

Rusty was ready for a break and, after that, excited about a car ride. I snapped him in the front seat doggie halter belt, and we headed home.

Dad's truck stood out on the driveway apron as both he and Mom unloaded gear. Tack and camping supplies went in the truck bed to be transported to the back barn for storage until spring. Mom and Dad would spend a day cleaning leather and fiber materials they had used. Dad was very tidy that way. It had become a ritual.

Mom glowed with the joy of living outdoors for the past week. Always smartly groomed with makeup that enhanced her appearance, the trail gave her the opportunity to relax and go bare-faced. This year, as always, she'd been the trail cook and had brought along her cast iron. Mom loved cooking on drives and enjoyed riding with her family. Some of the guests she helped shepherd became like family. She made friends easily.

As the high school rodeo queen many years ago, she had always loved being in the saddle. Every spring and fall, she and Dad helped Tom and Anna. Mom had ridden in every drive except when pregnant with me. Melody and I had helped through our school years until we both left for college. Tom's livelihood was primarily cattle, but he supplemented his income with a pack station business. Tom had his regular hands who worked the station in Mammoth Lakes during the summer but drives always required more help. Help came in the form of weekend cowboys who loved life in the backcountry. Their help was as welcome as the fees they paid to ride.

Dad was another matter. While he could ride as well as any of us, he was more of a bird and wildlife watcher. He was an L.L. Bean kind of guy. He loved the outdoors, but horses weren't his favorite mode of transportation. He rode with Mom and Tom because he loved them. Dad's brother died young in a motorcycle accident, and he missed the companionship a brother brings. Tom filled that place better than anyone could.

Dad wheeled out a dolly to load Mom's heavy cast-iron pans. It was easier to use the dolly than to carry them individually. She placed the last one on top of a pile of four and glanced up as I walked over. Sometimes when I saw these two together, my heart got so big it felt like it would burst with love. I so appreciated their love for each other and for me. After a decade of living without it, I savored every moment. I wanted to be like them when I grew up.

"Oh, honey. It's so good to see you." She grabbed me in a fierce embrace. "I smell like an old boot cooked in a campfire, but I've got to hug you."

I hugged her back, unwilling to give her up for the moment. I decided against warning them about Mark for now. There were variables that I couldn't predict, and I didn't want the Gibsons or the Murrays to worry unnecessarily.

From her back pocket, her phone chimed. She read the text and her eyebrows furrowed. "It's Anna. She needs your dad and me over at their house right away."

"Did she say why?"

Her ponytail swung as she speculated. "A problem with one of the horses maybe?"

Tom and Anna kept a pair of quarter horses on their property. They'd built a gate onto the adjoining cattle lease property. It was more convenient to have the two geldings in their backyard rather than driving down to south Bishop, catching, and loading horses to patrol property they could see from their backyard.

"You want me to come too?"

"Yes." She texted Anna back. Then to me, "Go get your dad, please. I'll get the truck started."

So much for my plan to wait. "Mom, you should

know that Mark came back to town this week. He's been waiting for Tom and Anna."

Mom glowered, one of the few times I'd ever seen her angry. Her hands flapped in a *shoo* gesture. I ran to get Dad.

❀

Moments later, the three of us piled out of Dad's truck at Tom and Anna's house. Tom's voice rose above another man's voice. "You have no business here. Leave, *now*."

Mark's voice had a whiny quality to it. "But you're my parents. I only want to talk. I'm your only child left."

That stunned everyone. Anna's face puckered in a horrified sob as she fell into Mom's arms. Tom's spine was ramrod straight as he said, "You hurt people, everyone, but mostly the ones who love... loved you. It's what you do."

Mark stepped back, surprised at the power of his father's words. He sputtered, "Dad, I never meant..."

Tom shook his head, his voice deepening with the power of his pain. "You may never mean to hurt us, but you do. You don't think of anyone but yourself."

Mark's eyes took on a haunted look, his hope looked to be fading. "How can I make it up to you?"

"No." Anna sobbed, her hands balled into tight fists as she squared off with her husband. "I won't have it, Tom. I can't let my child walk out of our lives."

"We can't trust him." Tom fixed a grave stare on his son. "I won't stand by and watch your heart being broken again."

"Tom," Anna pawed at her husband's broad chest. "He's right. He's the only child I have left. Melody is gone. But Mark is here. *Please*." Their tragedy revealed itself in her eyes, uncertainty in her quivering lip. She knew taking Mark back into their lives was risky.

Tom grasped his wife's hand and brought it to his lips for a soft kiss. He was silent, steeling himself. Then, after a long searching look at his son, Tom's brow furrowed. "I guess we need to do some talking, then." He dropped his wife's hand and curled it around her waist in a hug.

Silently, Anna took Mark's arm and steered him through the breezeway to the backyard. She pointed to an Adirondack chair and went out of sight. Tom followed.

Without a word, Dad and Mom walked to the truck, both their faces pinched with dread. I couldn't help but wonder what pain was in store for Mark's parents as I followed.

Chapter Thirty-Seven

I went back to work and checked on Javier. Libby was almost finished cleaning up, and I actually caught Marie humming to herself. Layers was operating fine. After turning the *open* sign to *closed*, I stayed with Javier until the till was counted out, then went upstairs to get ready for Reginald's funeral.

I changed into clothes I'd brought with me this morning. Clothes a bit dressier than what I was wearing was in order. It would hardly be fitting to show up at Reginald's funeral with a Layers shirt on. I washed my face, put on some mascara, and tucked my blouse into my skirt waistband. I looked in the mirror. That was as good as it got.

The funeral home was two blocks off Main Street. Arriving late by design, I parked two blocks away and walked. The home had many people attending, but not strained to capacity. It spoke volumes to me that with an established family who had been here for three generations, Reginald wasn't all that popular. I recognized several people, most of whom didn't recognize me.

Although I didn't feel I'd changed in the ten years I was away, this crowd proved otherwise. There was a small blessing in that it gave me the much-appreciated anonymity that I craved. I found a place standing near an archway to the outer room that led to the front door. A quick getaway is what I had in mind. I'd know when to leave.

At the podium, a speaker recapped the positives about Reginald's life. He droned on as I spotted Judith's bouffant hair. She sat up front with Devon next to her.

A baby fussed, was quieted, and then fussed again. The mother stood with an infant in her arms and made her way toward me. She smiled ruefully as she passed by, as if I'd know what she was dealing with. I didn't. I may have looked maternal, but I hadn't much experience with babies. Being an only child and the youngest of the cousins, I never changed diapers. While growing up, instead of babysitting, I got jobs feeding livestock and pets. Babies hadn't been on my radar.

Watching the mother comforting her child while strolling around the outer room, I got the most complete feeling of calm. I searched the baby's face, big cheeks, bright blue eyes, and dark hair, and found the reason of the mother's calm. The baby's smile became a treasure when her mother knew she was the reason for it. It was her child.

With a sudden stab of envy, I turned and left. This was not someplace I wanted to go. If I wanted this, I'd have to make meaningful changes. I couldn't take a risk with Jake. I hardly knew him. No way I would backtrack to Blaine.

Avoiding the young mother's curious gaze, I walked out into the bright afternoon sunshine and wiped away a tear.

Chapter Thirty-Eight

Sunday brought some much-needed calm. I missed Jake beside me at church and hoped he'd be back by next weekend. Sitting with Mom and Dad helped center my fragmented thoughts. While not necessarily reveling in the *Sensible Sarah* moniker, I prided myself on doing a decent job of managing my life. Yesterday's revelation set me on my heels. It was the first time I'd ever considered having a baby. I'd always pushed those thoughts out of my mind after considering Blaine as a father. Then viewing the sublime expression of peace on the young mother's face at the funeral, I began to think about it. Seriously.

Wesley's sermon played right into my ticking biological clock. To sum up a ten-minute homily, I came up with two sentences. "Let God be in charge. Trust in your maker, quit fighting his messages with your own spin." I wasn't doing such a great job on my own, anyway.

After the service, Emily spotted me and flagged me down. Dragging her husband over, she carried a baby in her other arm. "You remember Matt."

Matt Kilbride was a strapping rancher type, complete with Justin boots, a belt buckle the size of a garbage can lid, and a summer straw Stetson. His sunburned face broke into a smile as he greeted me. In high school, we had geometry and trigonometry together. Our shared memories of struggling through Miss Fletcher's class made our reunion that much warmer.

Emily continued, "And this is Hazel, our latest." The baby's dark eyes opened wide at this new stimulation. Me. The baby wobbled a bit as she struggled to hold up her head and focus on me. "She's five months tomorrow."

Matt wandered off to another clutch of people, having heard all the baby admiration stories before.

I touched the baby's soft cheek, and she cooed. Her head began to flop, and Emily's practiced hand braced her. The surprise in Emily's eyes faded as fast as it sparked. She'd seen I was interested in Hazel.

"You want to hold her?"

My heart swelled. "Oh, could I?"

Emily handed Hazel into my waiting arms, and I smelled the wonderous fragrance of baby. Part shampoo, part lotion, and a little perspiration. I positioned Hazel's head in the crook of my arm as Emily showed me. The baby's deep coffee-colored eyes watched me intently. I rocked her gently and said her name. A smile curled on her bow-shaped lips, and my heart jumped.

"Em, she likes me."

"Yes, she does." Em smiled broadly. "But it might be gas too."

"I don't care. She's precious."

"She is until she isn't. When she's hungry, or sleepy, or has full diapers, she's not so pleasant. This one's got a pair of lungs on her."

I traced a finger around her ear, and she smiled again. "She's an angel."

When I handed Hazel back to Emily, my arms felt strangely empty. "Why don't you guys stop by Layers on your way home? I'll treat you to some extravagant pastries. Our special today is pumpkin pie croissants." I prayed Tiffani had made it to work today.

"Thanks, we'll take you up on the offer." Emily didn't miss much. She leaned into me, the baby's hair brushing my shoulder. "You need one of your own, sweet Sarah."

I tried to laugh that off, but this was Emily. "Tick tock." she said. She knew me too well.

Chapter Thirty-Nine

Sunday morning at Layers was busy. The Mammoth crowd and fishermen were headed south to San Diego and Los Angeles. They often dropped by for a tasty breakfast to eat on the way home. Then there were the local after-church folks, like us. There were over a dozen people in the front, served, being served, and doctoring up their to-go coffees.

I entered through the back with Emily, Matt, and their family. From the baker's racks, I let them each pick out what they wanted. Thankfully, Em and hubby wanted only coffee, so I poured three cups and brought them back to the inactive worktable. Three little heads, two boys and a girl, bobbed over the desserts, relishing their treats. It wasn't long before raspberry jelly smeared all three faces and everything else within their arm's reach.

Matt stood and looked through the door to the front room. "There's Zeb. I wanna catch him. He's been dodging me all week about the irrigation on the south end." He put the cap on his coffee and headed toward Zeb.

"I'm glad he's gone. I want to say something, Sarah." Emily absently dabbed at Hazel's chin. Milk from her bottle had settled into a milk beard. "I know you don't think you're ready, but Sarah, you need to get on with your life. This bakery is a remarkable project, but it shouldn't hold you back from marrying and having a family. You were made for this. Look at your family."

I chewed my lip. What could I say? I'd been thinking the same way. "You know my Mom is one of the oldest families in the Owens Valley. In 1861 her great-great-grandfather Gibson came through herding cattle and horses for mining towns in Nevada. They found the area good for livestock, so they settled here and have been here as long as Europeans have."

Emily's eyebrows shot up. "I knew you had history here, but…"

"That history stops with me. So far. But I want more than a legacy."

Hazel picked at Emily's curls. "More than a legacy? Like what?"

I nodded, searching for the words. Emily was the safest person to tell my thoughts to. A lifelong friend, she'd proven her loyalty over and over. I wanted to tell her, to see how this sounded. Then I'd tell Jake.

"I want what my parents have, to put it bluntly." I reached over and took Hazel from her arms. Hazel's head bobbled until I caught it with my arm and stabilized her. "Mom was the high school rodeo queen the year dad moved to town. She was on the front page of the *Inyo Register* and everything. Dad had been recruited by the chamber of commerce to be the town optometrist. In those days, it was difficult to get professionals to stay here because Bishop is so remote. Dad's plan was to work his commitment of five years, then move back home to Reno. But the day he moved here, he saw her picture on the front page of the newspaper. He fell in love. Dad's parents were older, and not long after he moved here, his mother had a stroke. The family pressured him to return to Reno to care for her."

"But he knew his future lay in Bishop with the rodeo queen. They'd fallen in love. Mom was barely eighteen, and they were in love. But Dad's a responsible guy. His parents needed him. He found a temporary replacement optometrist for Bishop, deferred his recruitment, and returned to Reno for three years. His mom passed away. When he told his father he wanted to return to Bishop and marry Mom, well, Granddad wanted to be with his son. So, they sold the family home and moved to Bishop for good. Finally, Mom and Dad were free to marry. Granddad passed away the year after they moved, and I was born shortly after. Dad's replacement optometrist loved the area so much that he stayed on. Their partnership is still operating after almost forty years."

Emily sighed, and Hazel dozed on my shoulder. "What a love story. It's awesome that your mom waited for your dad. They must've truly been in love."

"They were. They still are." I focused on the baby. "I told you this story, so you'd know what kind of people I'm from. Responsibility and duty are words we live by. It's who I am. That's why people call me Sensible Sarah. I'm not spontaneous. I consider action I take."

"And Blaine? Where did he fit in?"

"Blaine was a mistake. I couldn't admit it for the longest time out of stubbornness."

"And what about Jake?" I'd told her about my interest in Wesley's brother. She hadn't yet met him.

"That remains to be seen. But it shows a lot of promise." I smiled at my friend. My own personal cheering section. "But the bottom line is that I want what they have. I want that person who thinks of me before himself. And I want to be that for my partner."

"I sure hope this Jake guy will meet your expectations."

"Me too, Em. Me too."

Chapter Forty

Monday morning dawned on McLaren Lane, and a new fall crispness to the air struck me as I stepped outside. It was cooler than yesterday. A few dappled yellow leaves interspersed with the green fluttered in the birch trees in the front yard. Usually, when the leaves turned, it started from the top and worked its way down. I loved being home where the seasons were so demonstrative.

In the kitchen, Dad was dressed for work in khakis and a blue oxford shirt, mulling over the world news on his iPad. He shut down his tablet, finished off his oatmeal, and put his spoon down, placing it carefully next to the empty bowl. He glanced at me and pushed his gold-rimmed glasses up his nose with an index finger. "Are you off to work, then?"

I poured a travel mug of coffee. "Yes, sir, as soon as I get my purse." Mom must have been out feeding the chickens. "You're up early."

He stood. "Can I have a minute?"

"Of course." I fixed the lid on the mug and faced him.

His normally lightly tanned complexion reddened. Uh-oh. He didn't like what he had to say. Was it time for me to move out? Had I overstayed my welcome?

He nodded outside, to where I saw Mom at the chicken coop. "She's worried about you, you know."

I nodded, waiting.

"We both are." He licked his lips. "Let the police do their jobs, Sarah. You don't need to prove your innocence. Not to us or anyone."

I sat down, staring at the top of my mug. "I know. It's almost like I can't control this insatiable curiosity. I know you and Mom must think I'm a meddling snoop." I had a hundred more justifications on the tip of my tongue, but the misery in his gaze stopped me.

"Sarah." Dad sat opposite me and took my hand in his warm grasp. "We treasure you beyond everything we have. But we saw what happened to Tom and Anna when Mark left. The aftermath of his disgrace almost did them in. I think your mom is afraid that this murder suspicion will overshadow your life, make you miserable, and in the long run, turn to hating Bishop and leaving."

"That could never happen. I left Bishop once but won't again." I thought of Jake and living somewhere other than here, together. I couldn't bear it. "This is my home. This is precisely why I want to know who killed Reginald. I don't want people whispering behind my back, wondering if I stabbed my competition."

"Never for a minute did we think you had anything to do with his murder." He pulled his hand back to his spoon, fidgeting. "Even though some of my patients have asked about you."

Horror grabbed my insides. "Oh no, Dad. I'm so sorry. That's exactly what I wanted to avoid."

"Oh, I don't give a rat's patoot about them. I'll defend you as long as I have breath."

"But you could lose patients, endanger your practice." There was an ugly ripple effect from my questions. They were touching and harming people I loved. I'd have to be more subtle.

He blinked, then shook his head. "I told them you found the body, that's all. And it's more than they need to know. If they want to find another optometrist, good riddance."

"You don't mean that. I know your practice is like your second family."

He watched Mom for a moment. "You're pretty darn precious to us, you know. We wanted more kids, but God had other plans. Now, with Melody's loss, I see how tenuous our grip on our children is." He covered my hand again with both of his. "Please be careful how you proceed."

"I promise I'll be mindful, Dad. I love you." I stood. With an eye on the kitchen clock, I realized it was time for me to leave for work.

He stood and put a strong, sinewy arm around me. "I love you, too, Sarah."

Chapter Forty-One

I left for work, mulling over my father's concerns. I should be more careful about asking questions—who, when, and where. Rusty and I hopped in the car and began our five-minute commute.

At Layers, I helped Javier at the front counter. Tiffani was late again, so I wrestled with the demonic espresso machine. I was more than pleased when I got a call from the police chief, Frank Scherwin, at ten o'clock.

"How about you come down to the station, and we have a chat?"

My heart thudded against my ribs. "Am I under arrest?"

He snorted. "No. We can meet for coffee at the café on Academy Street if you'd prefer?"

With a relieved sigh, I agreed. Javier gave me an indulgent smile when I asked if he could muddle through operating the espresso machine. I shook my head as he demonstrated a significant skill. It would be his job now when Tiffani was absent.

I let Rusty out for a break, grabbed my wallet, and

strolled the three blocks to the Academy Street Café in the bright sunshine. A brilliantly colored Fall Colors Festival poster greeted me in a window. The café is what Jake would call a woman's café. Quiches and frittatas were the café's specialty. They also featured pastries from Layers. The food was good, but much of the plate showed when served. Last time we ate here, Jake went to Burger King for lunch after the meal. I was fairly sure Frank felt the same way, but the place served wonderful coffees. And someone else operated the espresso machine.

Irene, the owner, greeted me as an old friend. We had met a few days ago to discuss her booth at the Fall Colors Festival. She was also on the board and was incredibly helpful both with ideas and materials. I'd found her to be a fun, well-traveled, and intelligent woman. Aside from Layers, this was my preferred coffee spot. At midmorning, we were the only customers. I pointed to a table in the far corner, and she led the way.

Our orders were easy, one coffee, black, and my favorite of the season, a simple pumpkin spice latte. That jogged my memory to change the window display to fall colors from the summertime motif.

Frank was a potbellied middle-aged man with an air of swagger. In the same gesture as his son, Cameron, he slipped off his straw cowboy hat. He wore a uniform shirt with jeans. I saw no sidearm. We'd crossed swords once in the recent past but had worked through it. He'd proven to be trustworthy. He was also Libby's boyfriend's dad.

"Was your woodin' trip successful?" There was no 'g' at the end of wooding. I guess it was an old-timer thing. "Did you get lots of firewood?"

He sat back with a grin. "Yep. Plenty of firewood."

"I read in the *Inyo Register* how Edison, the utility company, is subsidizing alternate ways of heating."

He nodded enthusiastically. "I converted to a pellet stove last year. I don't even have a place to burn firewood anymore." At my quizzical look, he explained. "I go woodin' for a couple of reasons. First, the firewood goes to a few families on the rez. They could use the help. The second reason is purely selfish. I get to spend some man-time with my son. We camp, cook, and work, either talking or not. But this might be the last time. He might not be around in a year or so when—and if—he goes to college."

I nodded, understanding, as our coffees arrived. Irene was discreet and left without a word. My respect increased for the man who wanted to maintain a relationship with his son. I thought of Tom Gibson. "So, what did you want to see me about?"

"I understand Foster brought you in for questioning about Reginald Bateau's homicide."

"He did." Not knowing the goal of his questions, I took a page from the unofficial trial testimony procedure for police. Answer simply, no embellishments, opinions, or emotions.

"You found the body?"

"I did."

"Foster said you were cooperative throughout the questioning."

"I'm glad he thought so." I certainly wanted to be cooperative, but Foster's attitude had made it difficult.

"He also said he thought you were holding something back." Frank blew across his steaming coffee with an eye on me.

A dart of irritation shot through me. That Foster

character was as unpleasant as they come. "I wasn't."
Then, I added mentally.

"That's an intriguing answer." He raised one eyebrow in a questioning slant.

"He probably picked up on my dislike for him."

"Sarah, we both know you're better than that." With a 'you-don't-want-me-to-believe-that' grin, he said, "I'll bet you're a darn good poker player."

"I don't play." My stomach churned. I didn't play poker, and I didn't like this dark alley he was going down.

"You know what I mean." He gave me a slow appraising glance. He leaned over the table and whispered, "What do you know? I'm sure you've been asking questions."

I thought for a moment. If I told him what I knew about Judith, Devon, Harlan Evers, and Larry Nixon, maybe that would be enough. Maybe I could make a deal with Frank. "How about I give you what I know if you do something for me?"

With a skeptical nod, he agreed. "Within reason."

"Call off your bulldog. Foster's spying on me for no reason." I hadn't seen him. It felt more like I sensed him keeping track of me.

"You're assuming I have control over him." He smirked. "All right. But if a lead comes up with you connected to it, he and I will be talking to you."

That was a reasonable concession. "We have a deal." I began, "Judith and Reginald weren't the happily married couple they made out. Judith said he watched every penny she spent. He controlled the finances but didn't do a good job of it. Judith hinted that they were having serious money problems. Devon, his son, was equally unhappy with his father. Devon didn't want to go to college as Reginald had planned. Reginald didn't have the cash to send his son to a university but insisted on it. Devon figures it was a prestige issue for his father."

Frank sat back; his eyebrows shot up in surprise. "That doesn't make sense. How does he figure he's going to pay for his son's education if he's got money trouble? I'm dealing with Cam's college expenses now, and they're expensive. Even with student loans."

"Think about it. Reginald was the Sunrise Club's biggest fundraiser for local education, so he'd look like a fool if his own son didn't go to college. Devon wanted to go to a vocational school and his high school counselor, Harlan Evers, supported that. Evers had literature sent to Devon at home, Reginald saw it and flipped out. He went to the school and yelled at Evers. I suspect he threatened Evers, but the counselor didn't give that up. I'm sure he's hiding something."

Frank blinked with amazement. "You've given me several people to check into. That's more than Foster has rounded up in a week." He leaned onto the table with a smile. "Do you want a job?"

"I'm not finished." I flashed what I hoped was a modest smile. "The banker, Larry Nixon, was evasive when I talked to him about Boulangerie." I explained the ruse I'd used to get information. "I understand confidentiality, but he cut me off when I mentioned the leverage he might have. He just about threw me out of his office." I leaned into the table and lowered my voice. "There's something there. Something he's not telling."

Frank's jaw dropped. He gawped for a second, then shut his mouth. "Holy cow, Sarah. This is very interesting stuff. I can work with this." He cocked his head sideways. "Or get Foster to do it."

I smiled, keeping the most compelling person of interest to myself. He was family, after all.

"Even with this information, you realize I can't clear you yet." He picked up a spoon and stirred his cold, black coffee. "Libby can't vouch for all the time before you left. She can't even say why you went to Boulangerie."

"Of course not. She was in the back, and I was in the front of the bakery."

He grimaced. "Olive at the sporting goods store was helpful, but that only accounts for a few minutes." He pulled the spoon out and carefully laid it beside his mug. "Your statement says you received a phone call from the manager at the bakery requesting you to respond because Reginald was going crazy."

"That's right."

"He said you were the only one who could calm Bateau down. Is that true?"

I felt like I had to be truly clear here. "It's true that Javier said that. I'm not sure it's true that I could calm Reginald down. I don't necessarily believe it."

He studied me acutely for a moment. "Are you telling me everything?"

"Yes." I widened my eyes, the picture of honesty. I couldn't tell him about Mark. Having Mark questioned by the police could jeopardize the possibility of a future with his parents. On the other hand, if I kept this to myself and it came out, the Gibsons might blame me for lying by omission. I loved those two people, almost as much as my own parents. Most of my life, they'd been there beside Mom and Dad... and Melody. How could I hurt them? There wasn't an easy way out of this dilemma. I wished I could talk it over with Jake. He'd have the law enforcement perspective and know whether Mark's arrival was pertinent or not.

But Jake had already weighed in. He'd said he didn't trust Mark. Neither did I.

"There is one more thing…"

Chapter Forty-Two

I t was lunchtime by the time Frank paid for the coffees and left for his office. I walked back to Layers, mulling over what I'd told Frank. It was the third week of August and still hot, but hints of fall were beginning to appear. In spite of my preoccupation, I couldn't help but notice the tree leaves changing, birds busily storing up winter food, and pickup trucks with beds full of firewood. All signaled the fall season was approaching.

I poked my head in at Layers. Javier was smiling at the front counter, helping a customer, Libby, Marie, and Charlie were in the kitchen, hustling between worktable and ovens. Javier said he'd already eaten his lunch, so he didn't need a break. The kitchen crew always managed lunch breaks themselves. I decided to get Rusty and go home for lunch. I needed some sane time with Mom.

I texted her, so Mom was ready with a sandwich and a small salad for lunch. I let Rusty out in the backyard and slipped into a chair at the kitchen table. I asked Mom about the horse drive, and she filled a half hour with tales of the trails. Like how Dad got lost coming back from a nature break, and Tom and Anna went swimming in their skivvies in an alpine lake. She hooted at the memory of them coming out of the water, their skin shriveled and blue from the cold.

I pushed the empty plate away. "Have you heard from Tom and Anna about how it's going with Mark?"

Mom bowed her head, her posture giving away her distress at the mention of Mark. "Anna's texted me that they're talking, but that's it. Dad said he hasn't heard from Tom." She slid into the chair beside me.

I had to tell her. I hated to burden Mom, but she should know. She knew Anna and Tom better than anyone. She'd know whether they could handle the news about Mark.

"Mom, there's something you should know. I'd like your opinion about whether Tom and Anna should be warned."

"It's Mark, isn't it?"

I nodded, not trusting my words yet.

"I knew it." She slapped the table. "I'm a mother, and I understand Anna's reasons, but Tom's got the right idea. He needs to protect her from their son. He's bad news."

I put my hands up to stop her protest. "Please listen. Maybe it's not as terrible as it could be."

Mom sat back, her face drawn and wary. "Okay."

"Mark came into town sometime before Reginald Bateau was killed. I don't know when. I haven't asked him. But he was at Layers with me when I got the call to come to Boulangerie. He left when I took the call. There was a twenty-minute gap between the phone call and my arrival."

Mom swallowed. "Twenty minutes is plenty of time

to drive up Main Street to Boulangerie, kill Reginald, and get away before you showed up."

"Right." I'd run this through already, driven and timed it. "Even if he drove side streets, he'd still have enough time."

"Who knows this?"

I paused. "Mark, me, you, and..." I winced. "...the police chief."

Mom sighed. "Then the lid is off this secret." Her clear blue eyes reached mine and held them. "You must tell Tom and Anna. If they find out you knew about this and didn't tell them, they'd never trust you again." She looked away. "As far as Mark goes, he's on his own. If he did this horrible act, he will have to pay for it."

I hurried to add the rest of the information. "There are at least four others who are persons of interest, so it may not be Mark at all."

"I hope not. Tom and Anna wouldn't be able to live with their only child as a murderer."

"There's one more thing. The police don't know this because I'm not sure it would help. One of my intern applicants saw someone shoot BBs at the museum camera that views Boulangerie."

"Oh." Her mouth dropped open. "The person who did that is most definitely the murderer, right?"

I grimaced, hedging my thoughts. "Not necessarily. This kid identified Mark Gibson's senior portrait from my high school yearbook. But," I had to talk over her protest. "But he also pointed to Ed Strange... you know Ed, he's Judith's brother. It's his picture that's right next to Mark's in an action shot during a basketball game." I shook my head. "It's far from conclusive, Mom. But more than nothing."

"Oh my God. You can't do anything with this. You take it to the police, and they'll have Mark frying. I don't trust him, but he's family. I think he's here to take what he can from Tom and Anna. Maybe not to hurt his parents intentionally, but that's Mark, totally self-serving. If the cops find the same breadcrumbs you have, they can have him. And Ed. Who would've even thought about him?"

"Right?" I folded my arms on the table and dropped my head on them. "What an ugly mess."

Mom stood up, as did I. It was time to get back to Layers to finish out the day. I'd text Anna to meet her and Tom after work this afternoon.

At the back door, Mom said, "Speaking of an ugly mess, look at your dog. He fell in the irrigation ditch again." With a tentative tail wag, Rusty waited to be allowed in—which of course, he wouldn't be. He'd fallen halfway in, his legs and rump wet with ditch water.

"What's that on his collar?" Mom opened the screen door and reached for a rolled up piece of paper, secured with a safety pin. We walked outside. Mom read the paper and looked at me with a gasp. I took the paper from Mom's trembling fingers.

No more questions. I warned you. You'll be sorry.

The paper fell to the concrete as I dropped to my knees. I threw my arms around my precious dog. I'd stop snooping if it ensured his safety. All the emotions of the past week caught up with me. The peril I'd put Rusty— and who else—in. A sob rose in my throat, and my mother's arms folded around me.

Chapter Forty-Three

Mom pulled me to my feet. "Let's go for a walk. Take Rusty. You need to calm down and think this through. And decide who you're going to call, the police or the sheriff." The murder was the police department's case, but the threat was received in the sheriff's jurisdiction. I would tell one and ask them to inform the other. There was no question in my mind or my mother's that this would be reported. I'll decide who first later. Right now, I needed to breathe.

A quick phone call to Layers assured me that Javier and Libby had matters well in hand. With Mark's return, Anna had begged off her counter shifts for this week. Javier was happy to have the extra hours. I told him I was taking the rest of the day off.

On the back patio, I leashed up Rusty and took him through the garage. There I found a bath towel to mop up excess water so he wouldn't become a mud ball. Out front, Mom tied her athletic shoelaces, then straightened with a grunt and took my arm. We walked down McLaren Lane toward South Mountain View, wandering from tree to bush at Rusty's whim. The road was wide and flat and easily traveled. Mostly we were silent as she let me ponder my issues through.

We were almost to Ranch Road, the street the Gibsons lived on, three blocks away, when I spoke. "I'll talk to Kelly. I trust him, and he'll let Frank Scherwin know if I ask him." I'd tucked the damp note in my pocket and was sure there was no chance of fingerprints, but I planned to hand it over anyway.

"That's only part of your problem, dear." She looked askance as we walked. "How are you going to keep Rusty and yourself out of trouble?"

"There's no easy answer to that, Mom. I can't let a murderer roam free, especially when I'm the prime suspect. The county school superintendent has suspended Better Off Baking until I've been exonerated. He thinks I could be a bad influence on the kids."

Mom huffed indignantly. "Those kids already are a bad influence…"

"Mom…" I stopped her protest. "The point is, we start with kids who need direction and discipline. That's a necessary element. This program can turn kids around. But me asking questions is more than that." I took a deep breath. "Remember how the Gibsons took such a beating to their standing in the community after Mark's… disaster?"

"Uh-hmm. It took them years to recover, even though they were an Owens Valley pioneer family. Most of these folks can't trace their lineage back two generations."

"Dad said something to me this morning that scared me."

"What was that, honey?" She stopped, knowing this was important. Rusty tugged at the lead, then sauntered over and sat by me.

"He said that a few people have already asked about my role in the murder. He said he minimized it as it should be, but I think he's afraid he may lose patients if... anything... more happens with me."

"Oh, I wish he hadn't told you that." Mom took my free hand. "I know you're applying this to what happened to Tom and Anna. I hope it doesn't happen to us, but we're bigger than this. Tom and Anna weathered their storm. So can we."

The thought of being arrested terrified me, both personally and for my family. I considered my blood relationship to the Gibsons. They would feel repercussions. I wondered if they could weather another storm if *I* was arrested. I kicked myself for being so self-centered. In the beginning, I'd worried about exonerating myself and finding the murderer. But now I realized how much bigger this whole dark cloud was. It could decimate the Gibson and the Murray families.

"Enough of that." I stopped and put my hand on her arm. "I want to hear more about your ride." She and Dad always loved the horse drives. They met the most interesting people in addition to working with old friends. The hands often returned year after year, springtime for the drive north to Mammoth Lakes and in the fall from Mammoth to winter pastures north of Independence.

Sensing my need for a distraction, she dove into her stories enthusiastically. "It was great. We had the usual mishaps, of course. It took one woman two wrecks before she figured the hands knew what they were talking about. She tried cutting through switchbacks." Shortening the trail by going off the established route can end with disaster.

"Yikes. Did she hurt the horse?"

She tipped her head in a slight negative. She usually

had a great attitude, usually a kindly humor about the flatlanders who paid to accompany them on horse drives. She blamed the trail rider for the injuries, rightfully. "He got roughed up a bit. But we treated his boo-boos and put the rider back on him. He made it through like a trooper, and the rider did better too. Tom was very patient—these people pay over a thousand dollars to get saddle sores, torn up by tree branches, sunburned, and chewed up by bugs."

I smiled, remembering the trail rides I'd been on. Funny that sunburns and bug bites fade in your memory, but the view from a sheer rock cliff to the valley below remains. It was scary the first time I went, but after a while, I learned to trust the horse, and I learned to follow the horse. They travel the same trails day in and day out. There were also beautiful cataracts falling over boulders, bouncing into pools, then draining downstream to another. The element of danger only added to the beauty of the places.

"Were there any problems with the timing?" Tom scheduled the drive three weeks earlier than usual due to predicted high winds and the possibility of wildfires.

"No, in fact, the grass, trees, and terrain were even prettier than usual just by going earlier. The leaves aren't turning yet, though."

"Well," I smiled and patted her hand. "At least you didn't lose anyone over the cliffs."

Chapter Forty-Four

We walked to the Gibson's on our way back from our meandering walk. Mom had texted Dad to bring pizza home for dinner as she was too busy to cook. We'd meet him there. A dutiful husband, he asked no questions. No doubt he knew he'd be filled in over dinner.

I was grateful that Mom would accompany me. Delivering this unwelcome news was going to be one of the toughest things I'd ever done. It would hurt Tom and Anna as well as endanger their marginally resuscitated relationship with their son.

Mark and his father were sitting in the backyard, gazing at the open pasture beyond their fenced property. The Los Angeles Department of Water and Power, commonly known around here as DWP, owned almost fifty percent of the Owens Valley land. A significant portion of that was leased to farmers and ranchers. The Gibsons' home sat on their privately owned border, with a view to their DWP cattle lease. Tom's family had managed the cattle lease property for years when Tom and Anna were able to buy and build their home on this lot in the seventies.

Anna handed us each a glass of iced tea and led us through to the backyard. I took Rusty off his leash, and he trotted around the yard, sniffing for interesting scents. Tom stood with a smile and toasted his beer to our tea in a welcome. Mark stood beside him, beer in hand also, and nodded to us each. Tom looked older; his face wizened from the sun, especially after his latest trail ride. His posture seemed more slumped, and his eyes drooped with what I saw as fatigue. He gestured to a pair of chairs nearby, and we sat.

Anna bustled into the house to check on dinner, but Mom called her back. "Anna, please come out here. Sarah has something that you should know."

I hated what I had to do. I don't *hate* often, but when I do, it's a strong emotion. I took a deep breath as Anna sat on the lounger next to Tom, his arm curling around her slim waist.

I twisted the leash handle around my finger. "There's no easy way to tell you this, but the police chief is going to be sending someone to talk to Mark."

Everyone looked at Mark, whose jaw dropped. "What? Why?" He dropped his beer bottle on the lawn.

I twisted the leash tighter. "The time when you got into Bishop is in question, Mark."

"You can't be serious." He looked from parent to parent, then back to me. "Who told you this?"

It was me who told them, but I didn't say that. This was brutal enough without the added element of a betrayed family loyalty. "You arrived at Layers at eleven. You left at eleven fifteen or so. I got to Boulangerie and discovered Reginald Bateau dead at eleven forty-five."

"Oh, I get it." His glare sliced me in half. "You think

because Bateau was a party to my sister's murder, I'd take out my revenge on him." He puffed his chest out with disbelief at the indignity.

The room was silent for a heartbeat. Tom spoke first. "Well, did you?"

Anna jumped up toward Tom as her son began his protest. "No, I won't let you ask him that, Tom. Please."

"Wait, wait. No, I want to answer this." Mark grabbed his mother's shoulder and pressed her beside him. "Listen, Dad."

Tom's face flushed, the vein in his temple throbbing. "I'm listening."

"I didn't do anything to Reginald Bateau. I couldn't if I'd wanted to." He looked at each of us as we waited for his alibi. "My car broke down, right in front of your bakery. It was there all day; I'm surprised you didn't see it."

Mom spoke up, the indignity of him attacking her daughter was too much. "She wouldn't have, would she? She discovered Reginald dead and had to go to the police department to defend herself." Mom wasn't convinced with Mark's excuse.

Mark looked at his shoes. "Oh yeah." But he had more to say. "But I had to call my buddy, Pete, to come pick me up. I hung out with him for a while until Wes came home."

Anna seemed eager to accept this. She glanced around, measuring the degree of doubt in the faces of her family. "Will your friend vouch for you?"

"Yeah, of course." Mark pulled out his phone. He scrolled through it and found what he wanted. He held out the screen for me to see. "Look, Sarah. You showed me the door at eleven fifteen. I went outside, and the steering in my car was busted. I called Pete for a tow at eleven twenty."

I looked but still wasn't sure. "All this says is that you called him." I let him figure out what he needed for an alibi.

"Well, if I have to. It's easy. I'll call him." He punched the screen. When a man's voice answered, Mark put him on speaker. Erratic metallic clanking sounded in the background. "Hey, Pete. I'm at home with my folks, and you're on speakerphone. They want to know when you came to get me on Tuesday and what we did all day."

"Yeah, buddy. Tuesday was the day the tie-rod broke on your car, and you had to be towed to Wilkerson. I was busy as a cat in a sandbox that day too. I was working on old man Murtagh's old International tractor. Remember when he taught us how to drive that dang thing?"

Tom straightened, suddenly looking as if a tourniquet had been released from his heart. "Pete? Pete Irving? From Irving Repairs out at Laws?" Laws was a small unincorporated community several miles northeast of Bishop. It has a noted railroad museum and old western movie sets but also housed some small industries such as a mechanic shop.

"Yeah? Hey, Tom, is that you?"

"Yes, Pete. It's me. You know it's my boy we're talking about?"

"Yeah, sure."

"He was with you all day?"

"Yes. I picked him up right away. I was down the street at my mom's place when he called. He helped me put together an old International Harvester. Took us all day. We was having fun rebuilding the tractor engine. Built in 1967, it was. Used real metal too. When we was done, he and I hauled his Chevy to Wilkerson. He said his cousin had tools and he'd work on the car later."

"Thanks, Pete. Glad he could help you out." A satisfied smile spread across Tom's face as Mark disconnected.

"Pete's an honest guy," Tom said to Anna, then Mom and me. "He wouldn't even *color* the truth to suit his own needs. I believe Mark did as he said. Besides, he's no murderer." He grasped Anna's outstretched hand. "We brought him up better than that."

Mark frowned, his eyes lasering in on me. "I can't believe you thought I'd kill someone."

Now came the second half of this challenging task—convincing Mark I spoke up for the family, not that I wanted to get him in trouble. His scowl told me I'd have to do a lot of explaining.

Chapter Forty-Five

"**M**ark, it's not that way…"

Mom's spine turned to steel as she stood to face Mark. "You might not know that the police are looking at Sarah as a suspect."

"So she throws me under the bus to get her off the hook? I see now." He looked at me like I was a pair of dirty field boots covered with manure.

"Mark…" Mom began until I put my hand on her arm to stop her.

This was my battle, not Mom's. "Can we talk about this? It's not the way you think. Let me explain."

"Explain what? How you've had it in for me since I walked the threshold of your precious bakery? Did you tell the folks how you practically threw me out?"

His question was rhetorical, of course. But now his assertion demanded an explanation. I faced the parents. "When Mark came in on Tuesday, you guys had just left. I thought he was here to stir up trouble over Melody's death."

Mark spat out the words. "Tell them what you said."

"I recall saying that Layers wasn't the place to tell you what happened to Mel. I recall telling you to meet me at my mom and dad's at two that afternoon. You never showed."

"I didn't have a way to get there."

Tom pulled Anna inside the house, with Mom following reluctantly. "Let the two of them hash this mess out. No reason for us to be listening in. It's between them."

"You know why now. My car broke down." Mark's whine grated in my ears.

"A phone call would've helped."

"Puleeze." He dragged the indignation out of each syllable. "It's been eleven years. I don't have your phone number."

I shook my head. "You always have an excuse."

"That's no reason to be rude to me, to refuse to tell me what happened to my sister."

"I merely postponed the news to a more secluded setting. You don't seem to understand that spilling the details of that horrible incident over again in the middle of a retail store isn't the right place."

"You didn't care about that. You liked the spectacular aspect of it, didn't you? Just like you enjoy being at the center of a murder investigation, right?"

He was talking Martian as far as I was concerned. I turned away. This was getting us nowhere fast. Once, I thought he'd known me, but not now. "You don't know me."

He grabbed my arm, trying to spin me around to face him. I stopped, my jaw set, and looked at his hand. Then into his furious eyes, I said, "Don't you touch me."

His hand dropped slowly as he realized he'd made a mistake.

"I don't care if you didn't murder Reginald Bateau." I squared off with him, meeting his awkward gaze. "I don't care what you do, except for when you hurt the people in our family." My hand swept the Gibson home. "When I saw you, I put my battle armor on to protect our family."

His shocked silence meant he was listening. Maybe a crumb of what I had to say would get through his thick skull.

"You have no idea of the debris you left behind in 2011 when you bailed on that girl. There was much more damage than the death of an innocent young woman. Her family broke up and moved away. They were unable to face anyone here in town because of the disgrace of her situation and your denial."

"I didn't... honest Sarah, I didn't..." he sputtered.

"That's right. Every sentence you utter begins with *I*. It's all about you. It always has been and always will be." I was fired up. I'd hoped to be able to face him someday and tell him what I thought. The time had come. The words I'd saved up after his abrupt departure had festered. He'd lanced the infection, and now all the ugly poison was pouring out. "Did you even think about your parents? They were left here to live with the shame you caused them. It almost killed them to see people turn away from them, embarrassed to be seen with them, to do business."

I took a breath as much for me as to give him an opportunity to speak. When nothing came, I went on. "As with all things, time distanced them from the debacle you'd left them with. Friends came around, people called on them again. Life returned to the Gibson household. But it took years. *Years*."

Mark's long hair hid his face. I couldn't see what was going on in his mind, as if I ever could. I finished up.

"And now you're back. How could you think I wouldn't warn them? I love them like they were my own parents."

I snapped the leash on Rusty's collar and walked out. I must've passed Tom and Anna in their home, but I didn't see them. I hoped they hadn't heard the butt-chewing I'd given their son.

Chapter Forty-Six

I was too darn angry to go home and be civil with the parents. I texted Mom and told her that Rusty and I were going for a walk, and I'd reheat a piece of pizza for dinner. She was relieved to hear from me, and I know she was anxious to find out how the "hash it out" went. But she had the good sense to wait until I processed it all myself. Maybe she should've been called *Sensible Meg*.

We'll be on Mumy Road for a walk. Be home soon. I sent the text and got both of us out of the car. The Camry was getting tired, and I'd vowed to buy a SUV before winter set in. Mammoth Lakes was up the road and well into snow country. I'd learned to snowboard a few years ago, and when I could afford it, I planned to buy a season pass. That meant driving in the snow and ice.

Bishop got snow every couple of years and never much. The annual average came in about eight inches, but the surrounding mountains got plenty. While a sedan was fine for highway or town driving in the summer and fall, getting around on the numerous graded dirt roads year-round would be easier in a four-wheel drive. My

penchant for hiking with Rusty had taken me to elevations where snow was an unexpected but frequent caller.
I loved taking Rusty out on the wonderfully graded
Forest Service roads that stitched through the desert and
into the mountains.

My favorite hikes were in the Buttermilk Mountains
off Highway 168. The dead-end highway led to a magnifi-
cent favorite among rock climbers, the area known for its
large "highball" boulders. I also loved Big Pine Canyon.
Its elevation began at seventy-six hundred feet, and our
favorite trail at eighty-six hundred feet. Rusty and I
frequented the Big Pine Creek Trail, but tonight was
getting late enough that the Sierra Mountain shadows
could be problematic. Some parts of the hike were
perched on the sides of nearly vertical cliffs that boasted
a thousand-foot elevation climb. Two hikers had fallen to
their deaths a few years ago. Trails were dicey enough in
the middle of the day, and I didn't have the energy to
tackle that tonight. Besides, it would be nightfall before
we ever got started, as it would require almost an hour's
drive to the base. Then hike for a while and another hour
drive back. Not today.

So, Mumy Lane it was. Flat, breezy, dry, and uninhab-
ited. Greeting us were the wide-open spaces of DWP
leases to the south or Bureau of Land Management property to the north and west.

I was settling down. Watching Rusty romping in the
desert and chasing sticks always lightened my mood. I
replayed the soundtrack of what I'd said to Mark and
concluded that I'd been pretty one-way about it. Especially after I accused him of being self-centered. I never
really gave him a chance to explain. But I still wasn't
clear why he returned. I know what he said, but he was
too vague for me to accept at face value.

But now, I savored my sweet Rusty. Although I'd owned him with Blaine for a couple of years, Blaine kept him until four months ago, when the dog's energy outlasted Blaine's patience. When we were married, living in Los Angeles, two years ago, a friend had sent me a bulletin from a local rescue about a found dog, a golden retriever/Irish setter mix. He'd been walking the shoulder of the Highway 5 onramp in Boyle Heights. A passerby picked him up before he got hit. He was only a puppy, but so big, they first thought he was full grown. He'd been named Rusty due to his reddish coloring. As he got older, the red faded to a beautiful rusty blond. I kept the name. My ex-husband, Blaine, had kept him after we separated. He had a more stable home as I planned on living with my parents for a while. I also thought he'd use Rusty as a bargaining chip for future contact. But when Rusty became unmanageable for Blaine, he called me to pick him up. With the caveat that I'd keep him forever, I was happy to pick him up. Blaine was embarking on a new romantic adventure and had no room for our dog. He agreed.

My phone chimed the Luke Combs song, *Better Together*, telling me Jake was calling.

I couldn't help but smile. "I was just thinking of you."

"I got the memo, so I called. What's going on?"

I sighed. "A lot of stuff. Nothing bad, not to me anyway. I'll fill you in later. Have you heard from the chief about Arco yet?"

I heard the smile in his voice. "Yeah, that's the reason I called. I wanted to tell you first. Arco's been retired, and I bought him for a dollar. He's mine now, Sarah."

"That's great. I'm so happy for you both." I closed my eyes and pictured Arco and Rusty racing through the sagebrush, chasing balls, sticks, and each other. "That's just wonderful."

He chatted on for a few minutes about department activities. It wasn't long before he asked about the Bateau homicide investigation. "Any news?"

"I talked to the chief on Monday. He still views me as a suspect, but mostly because my alibi isn't really definitive. He's called off Sergeant Foster anyway."

"That's something." He snickered. "What news did you have for the chief?"

I laid it out for him. I told him what I'd found out about Judith and Devon Bateau, Harlan Evers, and Larry Nixon.

"Sounds like you're still snooping, Sarah." His voice had a warning tone that I didn't take kindly to. I liked that he cared, but I didn't want to be controlled.

I decided not to tell him about the note I found on Rusty's collar. "It's not like that. People just talk to me. They always have. Really, except for the high school guidance counselor, they've all been contacts during the course of my day." Ewww, I stretched the truth on that one. "But the real news is about Mark."

"What about Mark?" Jake had taken an instant dislike to my cousin. I knew why, but I had to tell him about this afternoon's conversation. No, conversation isn't the right word. That implies two or more people talking. Mark never got a chance. I lambasted him up one side and down the other. For better or worse, I gave Jake the untarnished version of this afternoon's incident. It's better now that he knows how I can be when I get my righteous up.

At the end, he hooted and said, "I wish I'd been there, Sarah. I'd love to have seen you all fierce and indignant."

I smiled, tickled that he'd found it so amusing. We finished up with the details of his upcoming visit in two weeks. He'd been working to accumulate extra days off. The drive from Petaluma to Bishop took seven hours on a good day with no traffic and decent weather. He told me one trip he'd made after his wife died in December took him sixteen hours due to an unexpected blizzard.

"I'll see you then, Sarah. I'm looking forward to this time together."

"Me too. I love you."

We disconnected, and it occurred to me how unfair I was to Jake. I was making him wait for something I wasn't sure I could ever offer—myself. My marriage to Blaine had dissolved officially last month. Unofficially, I hadn't been in love with him for five years, at least. His dissolute ways, spending most of our income on flash, philandering, and outright lies, took its toll on my trust. Though Jake and Blaine were different people, I wasn't sure I could judge another person who was so close. Blaine certainly hadn't exhibited those characteristics before we married, or we never would have.

How could I know Jake would be any different? Maybe he wouldn't develop a gambling issue but maybe some other problem. I sighed, putting away my fears, and decided to examine my marriage and look at Jake for our future. While I couldn't predict behavior, at least with Jake, I felt like we would be able to talk it over.

That was already one point ahead of Blaine.

Chapter Forty-Seven

Tuesday morning dawned, a full week after Reginald Bateau's murder. A clear Sierra morning, with an early chill that promised to warm to the mid-nineties. Chief Scherwin had done the trick. Sergeant Foster hadn't bothered me once. I savored a cup of coffee in the backyard while Rusty sniffed the lawn and garden for the critters who'd passed by during the night.

My hours had changed since Javier's arrival. Anna was still off, and I had doubts about whether she'd return. But Javier had stepped into her position and taken on my counter time as well. The shop was making enough to pay full salaries to everyone. I paid myself minimum wage, and I needed to get back in the courtroom to be able to qualify for a loan to buy a new car. It would be after the new year, for sure.

When I arrived at Layers at eight o'clock, Libby was hard at work rolling out sugar cookies. She'd prepped the icing and colors, which sat out of her way on the opposite side of the worktable. Marie frosted a layer cake on the other side of the table, and Charlie was cleaning up after the morning's donuts, a mixed batch of raised donuts, fritters, and cinnamon buns. With everybody working nicely, I walked through and poked my head to the front counter. I found Javier talking to Tiffani. He showed her how to maximize the steamer on the espresso machine. God bless him.

I'd have to talk to Tiffani about being late and now seeing Javier helping her, the barista, made me wonder if I shouldn't let her go. While I didn't want to add to his workload—or mine—Tiffani didn't seem all that dependable. I'd talk to Javier about it later.

I ducked back into the kitchen and caught Libby's eye. She squealed and ran to me, startling Rusty. "I thought you'd never get here." She grabbed the sleeve of my sweatshirt and led me upstairs, Rusty trailing in bewilderment.

In the office, she bent to unleash Rusty and pulled out his bed. She pushed me down behind my desk and sat opposite. Her young face brightened with pleasure. "You cannot believe what's happened."

"Does it have to do with Cameron?"

"Yes." She seemed a bit disappointed that I'd guessed, so I stopped and listened.

"What?" She waited until I asked.

"Cam has asked me to be his partner. In a committed relationship. Like more than boyfriend and girlfriend."

I wasn't sure where this was supposed to go. "This sounds serious."

She nodded in agreement. "It is."

"But it's not an engagement?" I hated to ask, but I wanted to be sure.

"No. It's too soon for that." She twisted a turquoise ring on her finger. "I've got this job and school for the next few years. He's off to Cal Poly next month, looking at agricultural ecosystems or something like that. He's not sure yet."

Cal Poly was a California Polytechnic State University, a public university set on the coast in central California in the city of San Luis Obispo. Many Bishop kids went to Cal Poly for agriculture-related degrees as Bishop was a ranching community.

"It sounds like he's planning on making Bishop his home when he's finished with his education." This made me happy. So many kids went away to college bent on escaping the small town they'd grown up in. I'd done it and come to realize how much I needed to be here with my family. "How did your apartment hunting go?"

"Oh, I got it." Her eyes brilliant with anticipation. "It's not very big, but it'll just be me. I can afford the rent, so the owner had me fill out the paperwork. It's vacant now, so I'll move this weekend."

"This is thrilling, Libby." I wrapped my arms around her. "This is you starting over again, only making it better."

Her smile was sweet despite the nose ring and purple hair. I loved this girl. She'd come to be like a little sister to me. Melody had given her this job that saved her and began mentoring her. After Melody died, Libby let me take my cousin's place with little protest.

Libby's brow furrowed suddenly. "I am worried about maintaining a long-term relationship, though. I mean, my parents couldn't do it, and they're all I've ever known." She licked her dry lips.

I reached across the desk and grabbed her hand. "Libby, there's no template for a successful relationship. Sure, you can learn bad habits and traits, but all that can be managed or changed. I'm the worst person to give you advice on relationships. But you've got to hope and work at it." I thought of Jake. "Being able to talk through your troubles is key." I remembered Mom and Dad talking, sometimes with raised voices but not going to bed until they'd reached a solution. That's where I got my template of relationships. How I ever got sidetracked with Blaine, I'll never know. We hardly ever discussed anything important.

"Anyway, you two seem to be able to talk to each other. That's an attribute that should be nurtured, by both of you."

Libby stroked my hand. "Thank you for being my friend, Sarah."

"That works both ways, Lib. You're on the right path."

She hugged me as Rusty thumped his tail against his bed, looking from Libby to me.

Chapter Forty-Eight

"Good morning, Layers Bakery." It was already ten-fifteen the next morning. The time had flown by with unusually busy foot traffic. Libby's special orders had picked up as local families held parties for departing college freshmen. Harvest celebrations were right around the corner, and Bishop residents loved a reason to celebrate. Javier had the day off, so I worked the front counter and wrestled with the demonic espresso machine.

"May I speak to Sarah Murray, please? This is Larry Nixon from the Owens Valley Bank."

"Larry, it's me, Sarah. What can I do for you today?"

"Your expansion loan has been granted. You can come in today to sign the papers if you'd like."

What? "Larry, I thought you suspended the loan request after my last visit."

"I thought I had too. But it must have slipped through the cracks."

What to do? No way could I afford to buy Boulangerie. As far as I knew, Judith hadn't even made up her mind about selling yet.

"Well, that could be a blessing in disguise, Larry. I haven't heard from Judith about selling. I can't stop progress in my own house, so I'll be in to sign the papers in…" I glanced at the wall clock, ten-fifteen. I could get Charlie to cover the front counter. Rusty would need a break but couldn't wait in the car. It was still too hot during the day. "In fifteen minutes."

Fifteen minutes later, I scooted the chair under the extended lip of Larry Nixon's desk. He sat kitty-corner to me and explained each page, directing me where to sign. By these terms, I'd have the loan paid back in two years with minimal impact on profits. I could even afford to raise Javier's pay to almost what he made at Boulangerie. I was pleased with the overall financial health of the bakery. The expansion would add more to the daily receipts. There was enough business to support a café in the southern end of town.

Larry stood, picked up the papers, and called for his assistant to come into the office. She took the paperwork and said she'd return with my copies in a few minutes. For an awkward moment, I wondered what I'd say to Larry Nixon in the interim.

He cleared his throat and turned to close the door. He sank into his plush chair. I guess he felt equally awkward. This seemed to be the time to give it one last try. "I'm glad we have these few minutes. I'd like to clear up a misconception."

Like the fact that we'd both lied last visit. "Oh?"

"I have an admission to make. My version of the

conversation with Judith Bateau was slightly different than I portrayed. While she doesn't know what to do about the business, she made no overtures to me about buying Boulangerie." I twisted the handle of my purse. "In truth, Larry, I don't have the means to buy the bakery."

He sighed, focused on something over my shoulder. Maybe honesty was the trick to getting him to reveal how much pressure Reginald exerted on him. "In light of your frankness," he adjusted his gaze to me. "I feel compelled to do the same. But only to you. I don't like lying, and I found myself doing just that when you were in last." He pulled out a handkerchief and mopped his brow. Who carried a handkerchief these days?

"Go on."

"Reginald was pressuring me into holding off on fore-closure of the bakery."

"Foreclosure?" My arms blossomed with goose-bumps. "How could the business have gotten so bad? I worked there for several weeks this spring, and Boulan-gerie took in plenty of money."

Nixon pulled open his desk drawer and moved what sounded like papers around inside. "Oh, it wasn't the amount of money they took in. It was how much Regi-nald took out." He shut the drawer and sat back into his chair. "Reginald was a bit of a gambler. Usually online, but often Reno and Carson City as they're so close." Carson City was the capital of Nevada and a three hour drive north on Highway 395. Reno was another half hour in the same direction. Both had gambling machines everywhere besides casinos, including supermarkets and gas stations.

"He gambled away the bakery without his mother

knowing? She just passed away this spring." His gambling must have been going on long before she died.

Nixon's mouth twisted with disgust. "Two years ago, he brought me loan paperwork with his mother's signature. The contract used Boulangerie as collateral for a loan. I didn't look closely and later found that he'd forged her signature."

"Go on." I wasn't sure how this would coerce Nixon into looking the other way.

Nixon leaned forward, elbows on his desk. "When I called him on it, he threatened me. You see, he'd done the same thing five years back. I realized it, and when I called him on it, he convinced me to look the other way."

"Oh no."

"Right. He'd set the hook. I'd done it once, so why not again? He blackmailed me over the first incident. He knew he'd get in trouble, but he'd drag me down too. I couldn't have that. I have four kids, three in college, and one's getting married next month."

"You took money from him?"

Larry Nixon hung his head like a six-year-old caught pulling the wings off flies.

"It wasn't much at first, but the more ignoring he needed, the more he was willing to throw money at me to keep me quiet."

"How much do you think over the years?" It didn't matter, really. He'd get his due.

I let his shrug pass.

"You aren't going to tell anyone, are you?"

"I don't know what I'm going to do with this. Right now, I have to think of the relevance to the homicide investigation—it gives you a motive to shut Reginald up."

He groaned. "That makes me a suspect in his murder."

"But I'm not a cop. In fact, the police are less than happy there are so many people talking to me instead of them. So I'll just keep it to myself for now."

Chapter Forty-Nine

O n my way back to the bakery, my phone chimed the 1976 Don Williams country classic *Till the Rivers All Run Dry*, Mom's ringtone. "Hey, Mom."

"Sarah, it's Mark." My heart sunk, expecting all the worst-case scenarios had come true. He'd done something horrible.

"Oh no..."

"He's in the hospital. His car fell on him, Sarah. Oh, my Lord." Mom was in danger of blathering. I couldn't remember when I'd heard her so shaken.

"How did a car fall on him, Mom?"

"It was at Wesley's place. He was working on that rental car, and it fell on him."

She was so rattled; I knew that was all I'd get from her. "You want me to pick you up? Are Tom and Anna with him yet?"

"No, Anna just called. I was going to pick her up, but I can't find my car keys."

"I'll pick you both up, and we'll go to the hospital. I'm on my way."

I had a feeling of déjà vu when I pulled into the hospital parking lot. The memory of the night I'd found Melody, almost dead, then in Northern Inyo Hospital's hallways later when she died.

Tom's pickup was in the lot, and Anna jumped out of the Camry and practically ran into the emergency room entrance. Mom and I followed closely, watching out for her. Anna rushed into Tom's arms in the ER lobby. We stood by, not wanting to interrupt them.

Finally, Tom looked over his wife's head and said, "He's going into surgery now. His car fell on him while he was underneath working on it."

Mom and I nodded, not asking any questions. We all were acutely aware that a mere four months ago, we were here for their other child. Mom steered Anna toward a waiting room chair, and we all sat.

Ten minutes later, Wesley lurched out of an exam room. Pale and rumpled, with grease streaks on his face and hands, he faced Tom. He spoke in almost a whisper, but we all heard him. "They're taking him in now."

The two men sat opposite us. Wesley rounded up his courage. "Mark had parked his car in my driveway until he replaced the broken tie-rod. I came home a little early today, thank God. It looked like one of the jacks failed, and the blocks on the rear tires weren't secure."

Tom's forehead furrowed. He'd worked on cars and farm equipment with Mark during our childhood. I knew he was a safety nut, and this kind of apparent carelessness grated on him.

"When I got there, I think he'd been there for a little while. His shoulder and arm were partly pinned, and his face got banged up. He wasn't talking much sense, so I secured the blocks and looked for something to jack that side of the car up with. I found the jack that kicked out. I had one of my own, so I dug it out and used it. I'd called 911 when I found him, and the ambulance arrived as I pulled him out." Wide-eyed and looking bewildered, his gaze went to each of our faces. Wesley was a volunteer on the Inyo County search and rescue team. If he was waiting for judgment, he wouldn't get it.

Mom rose and went to him. She knew a maternal embrace was called for, and she was just the woman for the job. Finally, Wesley sobbed.

I wondered how much more this family could take.

Chapter Fifty

M ark was to be admitted. The doctor told Tom and Anna that there were more tests to run to be sure he hadn't suffered any internal injuries. After the surgery on his arm, Mark cleared post-op and was moved to a shared room with another. After he'd gotten settled in, Tom and Anna were allowed to see him. Tom left shortly afterwards, leaving Anna to sit beside their son in a vigil.

With dark shadows around his eyes, Tom passed us silently and walked up to Wesley. He nodded toward the door, and Wesley stood in a daze and followed. Tom stopped at the door and looked over his shoulder. "Thanks, you two, for being here." He paused. "Anna needs you both." He left, visibly troubled. There were several issues that could be at the heart of his concerns. I could do nothing for any of them.

I tugged on Mom's sleeve. "Let's go see Mark."

The room was quiet when we entered. A wall-mounted television with no sound played *I Love Lucy* reruns. Mark's roommate was a sleeping, aged Native

American man, either Paiute or Shoshone, as the reservation was less than a mile away. Anna sat beside Mark's bed, his hand in hers. The other hand had a tube inserted with a clear liquid flowing from a bag hanging from an aluminum stand. I stood, stunned at the sight of my cousin lying in a hospital bed with tubes inserted in him. He looked so much like Melody when his face was relaxed as it was now. With his drooping eyelids, I wasn't sure if he was fully awake. His left shoulder was bandaged, the arm suspended in a sling. Scratches covered his face, and a fist-sized bruise colored his cheek. He rested his left leg on top of the sheet, scratches and cuts doused with iodine all the way to his toes. This accident had been serious.

Anna saw me looking at the arm. "They'll cast it when the swelling goes down."

I nodded.

"Ice." Mark's voice was a notch above a whisper. Anna dropped his hand and reached for a cup of ice chips. She spooned a teaspoonful on his lips. When he'd finished, he gave his mother a halfhearted smile of thanks. "I wanna talk to Sarah."

With red-rimmed eyes, Anna looked up at me. She'd been there when I had laid into Mark. I nodded. Mom reached to her sister-in-law and offered to buy her a cup of coffee at the coffee wagon next door.

When they were gone, Mark shifted to his uninjured elbow and tried to lift his body upward to lean against the pillow. I tucked a pillow behind him, then another, and sat in Anna's chair. He wasn't vertical, but at least his upper body was on an incline. He could see me without a struggle.

I settled him in, tucking loose sheets and making sure the IV was still attached.

His voice seemed stronger than earlier, although it was still an effort to talk. "Thanks, Sarah."

"Of course."

"I want to tell you why I came back."

"Shhh. You don't need to…"

"I do." He took a deep breath, then spoke. "I know leaving the first time was wrong. I was being selfish, looking at it like my life would be over if I married her."

"You were young…"

Mark's eyes were wide open, the crystalline blue gaze cutting through me like it used to. "No excuses, Sarah. What I did was wrong, and it damaged two families, maybe more."

I couldn't dispute that.

"When I was in Mexico, I learned a lot about people and myself. The Mexicans who worked for me taught me humility. These people work—they dig and scrape for enough food to put in their dinner pot. They don't get caught up in partying or self-indulgence. They have a duty to their families to provide. So they do just that." His head dropped back on the pillows. This was taking a lot out of him.

"Admirable."

"Yeah," he said, staring at the ceiling. After a moment's rest, he eyed me again. "When my foreman invited me to dinner at his house one night last year, it changed my life. I'd suspected how they lived but never admitted it to myself." The man in the next bed began to snore. "Jalo's home was immaculate. No junk on the counters, nothing out of place. Four energetic, obedient kids all helped with the meal preparation. His wife Octavia served us a stew, goat stew it was. I speak enough Spanish to get the fieldwork done, but they didn't speak English. Their oldest son learned English in school. So that his parents wouldn't understand, he told me in English that the stew they served was their only goat. It had been used for milk and cheese. But they slaughtered it when I came to dinner."

Tears formed in his eyes. "And they were happy to do it. Hospitality and sharing what they had is a way of life for them. When I left, I couldn't help but apply what I'd seen to my selfish life."

I sat stunned at the lesson my cousin learned. I could only listen.

"It took me three years, but I converted the marijuana crops over to wheat, beans, and tomatoes. I knew I had to come back here to see Mom and Dad, so I put the farm up for sale and made sure the new buyer understood the culture down there. I wanted to protect Jalo and Octavia. But I had to come back to Bishop and try to make it up to Mom and Dad. When I got word about Melody..." He broke off, the words suddenly not there. He was still grieving for his sister.

"That's a remarkable story, Mark." I looked into his beautiful blue eyes. "I believe you."

"Melody made everything more important. I had to get back."

"Now you're here." I smiled at him.

"And somebody's trying to kill me."

I sputtered, struggling with the words. "What are you talking about?"

"Go to the closet and see if my jeans are there."

The closet held a transparent plastic bag with the hospital emblem on it. Inside, I found his wallet, car keys, and phone. "No jeans. They must've cut them off you."

"Check my wallet."

Opening his wallet, I found his Mexican ID card, thirty-two US dollars, and a folded scrap of paper.

"That's it," he pointed at the note. "Read it."

You're a victim of Sarah's meddling.

I dropped to a chair and put my head between my knees.

Chapter Fifty-One

Mark hit his controller for assistance. A nurse and an attendant rushed into the room, headed for the patient's bed. Mark's harsh voice repeated, "Her, not me."

The pair detoured when they spotted me. Embarrassed to my core, I pushed them aside and sat up. "I'm fine, I'm fine. I just had a shock. I'm fine."

Mom and Anna returned from their coffee break. Without missing a beat, they took over for the professional staff. With Mom's insistence, *I'm her mother,* they left.

When I could find words, I spoke. "Mark's accident wasn't an accident." I passed the note to Mom, who showed it to Anna.

"Oh, my Lord."

I'm not sure who said it, but the exclamation summed up my surprise. I'd been reckless with other people's lives. Oh my. Oh *my.*

Anna caught the implication immediately and called the sheriff. Mark's incident occurred in Wilkerson, outside of Bishop city limits, and the threat was found there, making it the sheriff's jurisdiction. Before the deputy arrived, the BPD detective Mitch Foster came in.

"Ladies, sir." He nodded to the room without making eye contact with anyone. "I hear there's been a threatening note found."

I wanted to tell him to butt out but didn't. "This all happened in Wilkerson." In other words, you can leave now. He encouraged Mom and Anna to find another place to sit for a while.

Deputy Truelove, a burly Native American version of my friend Kelly, arrived and took over the interview. Foster introduced him to me but had to ask who Mark was. "You're Mark Gibson? And you're related to the Gibsons how?"

"I'm Melody's brother."

Foster jumped on that. "Where were you when she died? I didn't see you at the funeral."

"I was living in Mexico at the time, and I didn't hear until afterwards." Mark was getting pale, his face drawn from fatigue and trauma.

Truelove spoke up to Foster. "I'll get what I need, then he's yours."

Foster snorted in agreement.

After taking Mark's basic information—which included his parents' place for his home address—Truelove asked about the incident. Mark was tiring and gave a concise version but ended with, "I didn't see who kicked out the jack. Nobody said anything. I heard metal against metal, like a crowbar hitting the jack. Then, I got pinned." I liked the way the deputy looked and listened before he spoke. His dark eyes were alert and observant.

"You didn't hear or see anything after that?"

Mark hesitated. He tipped his chin at me. "This note

dropped on the floor where I could get to it. So I grabbed it with my good hand and stuck it in my jeans pocket with my wallet."

I handed the note to the deputy. He gave me a quick, appraising glance, then again after he read it. "You're Sarah?"

"That's me." My voice sounded so little. I wished I could shrink to the size of an ant and crawl through a crack to disappear.

"What's this about, Sarah?"

"This relates to Reginald Bateau's homicide. I guess that's why he's here." I jutted my chin toward Foster. "I've been asking people questions. I grew up here and know a lot of folks. They know I'm local, so they talk to me." His face blank, Truelove looked at Foster. Foster curled his lip. Truelove looked back at me.

I shrugged. It sounded lame to me too. "Someone doesn't like it."

Truelove sighed and handed me his notepad. "I need the names of all those you've spoken to."

Beginning with Judith and Devon Bateau, I listed Harlan Evers and Larry Nixon. No one would be happy about being reported to the sheriff's office. But could one of those people be threatened enough by my questions to attack Mark? That was a question for Deputy Truelove. I felt comfortable that he'd be diligent about finding who.

Deputy Truelove thanked me for the information. He bowed his head slightly at Mark, saying that he'd be in touch, and left. I thought it significant that he didn't say goodbye to Foster.

Sergeant Mitch Foster had written answers from Truelove's questions. However, the deputy hadn't shared the names I wrote down in his notebook. Foster wanted those names.

He pulled out his notebook and pen. "Who did you speak to about the Bateau homicide?"

"I'll get the names to you tomorrow." Then to my cousin, I said, "Mark, I'll see you in the morning." I turned and left Foster sputtering behind me.

Chapter Fifty-Two

I didn't go far. Around the corner, I texted Charlie to have someone let Rusty out for a break then bring him back to the office. With a bowl of water and the air conditioning, he'd be safe there.

I leaned against the wall outside Mark's room. Foster's voice carried nicely. I heard it all.

"When did you hear about your sister's death?"

"Not until Saturday, August thirteenth. I couldn't get a flight out until Sunday, the fourteenth."

"You didn't drive?"

"I flew into LAX, then hired a Rent-a-Wreck. That pile of junk broke down on me. Tie-rod bolt sheared off so I couldn't steer."

"When exactly did you drive into Bishop?"

"Tuesday, August sixteenth. I dropped in to see Sarah at about eleven in the morning."

"What do you know about your sister's murder?"

"I know that she was in Wilkerson at home. Her brother-in-law's dog ran off, and she went out looking for him. The way I heard it, Reginald Bateau found her, and they argued about her bakery being competition for Bateau's. She fell, or he knocked her down and left her in the desert. Some other guy came by, found her, and killed her because he thought she knew that he'd killed his wife ten years ago."

"That about sums it up." Foster's voice softened. "Did you feel that Reginald Bateau was in some way responsible for your sister's death?"

Mark snorted. "Well yeah. If she hadn't been knocked out in the first place, the second guy couldn't have killed her. Of course, Bateau had a hand in her murder."

"Okay." I could almost hear Foster salivating at the prospect of another suspect. "Can you tell me where you were between eleven fifteen and eleven forty on August sixteenth?"

"Yeah. The tie-rod on my Rent-a-Wreck tweaked. Can't steer without it, so I called my buddy for a tow to Wilkerson."

"What's your friend's name and contact information?"

I'd heard enough. Pete Irving would alibi Mark and Foster would move back to me.

I'd gotten a text from Charlie about Rusty and was in the process of replying when I heard Foster say, "Don't go anywhere."

Mark guffawed. "Are you kidding? You're afraid I'll hobble back to Mexico? I can't even walk across the room."

The noise of the emergency room doors closing blocked out Foster's response, but I was with Mark. I let out a belly laugh at Foster's absurdity.

Chapter Fifty-Three

I went back to the bakery, liberated my sweet puppy, and headed home. We walked down Mumy Lane for a little stretch of the leg. Later, dinner with Mom and Dad was filled with questions and speculation about Mark's future in Bishop. I told them I didn't think he had anything to worry about. I didn't say that I'd been surprised before.

The next day after I'd contracted with three different vendors for the festival food tables, Libby, Marie, and Charlie got busy filling orders. Bishop was easing into harvest season, which was always a great reason for a gathering and cake. Kids going away for school, beginning a milestone grade, or teachers returning to the classroom were all celebrated in this town. Business was good.

To my surprise, Anna had returned to work, allowing Javier two consecutive days off and more freedom for me. It was time to jumpstart my real career, time to take steps to get back to the courtroom. A trip to Inyo County Personnel Department in Independence was on my agenda this morning. My second item was to meet Javier this afternoon and formally offer him the position of manager when I go back to court reporting.

The lovely human resources specialist in Independence was helpful. She took all the documents I'd been required to submit and set an appointment for the department manager to discuss the final details, including a start date.

I was vibrating with excitement when I got back in the Camry. I hadn't realized how much I missed my career. A few miles north and I figured out the tingle of excitement was mixed with hunger. I stopped in Big Pine for a chicken salad sandwich, ate it, and headed north. I was glad I'd left Rusty at home. Using voice command, I called Javier's cell.

He answered and suggested I meet him at City Park in Bishop. His niece was celebrating her sixth birthday—with cupcakes from Layers, of course—and he'd be in the back picnic area all afternoon.

The day was warm but not as hot as it had been. Still, as I got close enough to see them, the dozen six-year-olds displayed beads of sweat on their eager, joy-filled faces. Running, chasing each other, squealing with innocent delight, the scene made me smile. The adults stood chatting with each other over salsa music, laughing at their children, serving, and eating food.

Javier waved to me from the middle of a crowd. I'd never have seen him without the signal. He strolled to meet me, and we sat at a table some distance from the group. "What a great party. Your niece will surely remember this birthday."

Javier's broad face opened with the serene smile of a happy man. "We always celebrate birthdays like this. We honor our children."

"They're truly blessed." I turned my head, not daring to spend time looking at the little six-year-old girl in a pink princess dress. She was a beauty with the open-faced innocence of a child who'd not yet discovered a mirror.

At Javier's nod, I launched into the reason for the meeting. "I wanted to talk to you here because I need ten minutes of your time uninterrupted. The bakery is busy with staff and customers."

His tanned face grew serious, and I saw the premature lines around his eyes. Reginald Bateau's existence and death had a cost to others. Javier was still paying. He was bracing himself for being fired. We found a picnic table far enough away to afford us some privacy.

"How would you feel about managing Layers Bakery and Café full-time at the beginning of next year? I believe I can offer you the same salary that you earned at Boulangerie. And this will begin next January when I go back to work at the courts." I hadn't been given a start date, but January had been discussed. And the salary I offered Javier seemed generous but wasn't necessarily. Layers was a much smaller bakery, and Reginald had been notoriously cheap. Balancing the two factors out, I came to a reasonable figure. "You might have to put up with some construction, but I hope to have the café running by then."

His shoulders sank with what looked like relief. His thumb and index fingers rubbed his forehead. "Yes. This is what I hoped for." When he finally looked at me, his eyes had filled with unshed tears. "I'm very grateful to you and the bakery. Everyone's been so good to me."

"We believe in treating everyone with respect." His gratitude moved me deeply. I was amazed at the depth of harm that Reginald had spread. His emotional abuse and bullying had spread to Boulangerie. "I have another question. Why did you call me that day? I mean, you said Reginald listens to me. That's not been my experience. What made you say that?"

"Because he's always saying, 'when Sarah was here, you did it this way.' Or 'Sarah knew how to do this, why don't you?'" Making a third party the hero made no sense to me. Especially from someone who had to be the center of attention. Reginald wasn't thinking straight. I'd seen the results of his tirade. But someone else wanted to shut him down.

An ugly thought blossomed. Javier left after calling me for help the morning Reginald was killed. Javier might have been one of the last people to see him alive. "Javier, have the police been to speak to you?"

He nodded, leaning over clasped hands. "Yes, a sergeant. He was disrespectful, asked a lot of questions, the same one in different ways. He was looking for a reason that I would want to kill my boss. I didn't give him one."

"Did he make you account for your time?"

Javier's head bobbed. "Every minute."

"Did he come talk to you at your home, or did he make you go to the police station?" I wasn't sure if it was true, but I suspected Foster would try to intimidate Javier by reporting to the PD. Foster was shaping up to be a bully in my book.

"The police station." Javier sighed and sat back. "But the truth is the truth, no matter how many times it's asked or where. He had no reason to keep me."

Javier had never been a suspect in my mind. I suppose it's because I knew him well enough to judge his character. I hadn't been wrong. I'd been wrong about Mark, but that was different. He had history.

Javier glanced at his family. He stood, waving to someone. A sturdy-looking Hispanic woman with long black hair waved back and sauntered over to us. He introduced her to me. "This is my wife, Rosalia."

"*Con mucho gusto.*" she extended her hand to meet mine.

"This is my boss at Layers, Sarah Murray. She has just offered me a full-time manager position."

Rosalia hugged her delight to Javier. She patted him on the shoulder and shouted, "Go, go tell your brother. He will be so happy."

"Thank you, Sarah. I'll do a good job." Javier shook my hand, turned, and trotted over to his family.

Rosalia smiled beside me, obviously proud of her husband. "He's a good man. He deserves this chance."

"Yes, he does. He's earned it."

"There's much good about him that he doesn't tell. He doesn't like people to know his business."

"That's the definition of charity, I believe."

Rosalia's face had the same open honesty that I valued in Javier. "Did you know that Javier supports his brother and his family too?"

"No." I thought of the financial burden it must have placed on Javier and his family. "What a kind soul he is."

Rosalia's eyes narrowed. "His brother worked in the big bakery too. His hand got caught in a machine at Boulangerie. He couldn't work no more, so Mister Bateau fired him."

My hackles rose. "There's a law against that."

"Yes, but he'd have to hire a lawyer, and that takes money. We don't make that kind of wages. Mister Bateau knew that."

My anger grew against Reginald Bateau. The longer he was gone, the more stories like this surfaced. I shook my head in sympathy, considering resources. "Do you go to church?"

"Yes, Our Lady of Perpetual Help on Home Street."

I knew the church. "I have an idea. Check with Father Gracey and tell him about Javier's brother. He may know of some group that can help him."

Rosalia held my hand when she said thank you. My heart swelled at the pleasure to be back home where touching peoples' lives was done with joy.

I hugged her with an equal amount of delight.

Chapter Fifty-Four

After scouting several areas within the park for the festival, I got back in the Camry. As I headed back to Layers, Anna texted me, saying Mark was being released today. When I got there, I hurried through the kitchen and shooed her out. Even though Tom would pick Mark up, Anna would want to be at home to help her son.

With Tiffani on the espresso machine, I was happy to work the counter. Another half dozen special orders came in. Completed cakes and goodies were picked up. The day was flying by. Late last week, I'd posted a sign on the door extending our hours for customer convenience. Libby's friend had updated the website, and the hour between two and three o'clock were busy enough to continue for another week.

Three o'clock came around, and as I counted cash at the register, Tiffani strolled to the front door to lock it and flip the *open* sign to *closed*. A reedy, middle-aged woman with a Tilley hat, long-sleeved sun shirt, and pants pushed the door open, nearly knocking Tiffani over.

From the counter, I shouted as nicely as I could. "We're closed, ma'am. We'll be open…"

"I don't care what your hours are." She leaned over the counter, so I shut the cash drawer.

"Wait a minute, ma'am."

"No. You wait." Her flushed face went a deeper red. "You're responsible for this mess. If you hadn't…"

"Wait. What mess? I don't have a clue what you're talking about."

"You shouldn't have opened your big mouth, Sarah Murray. Reginald Bateau, that's what." The woman looped her arms across her flat chest. "You started this when you killed him."

I moved around the counter to face her. "I didn't kill anyone. Who are you, anyway?"

"You killed him as sure as I'm standing right here."

"You won't be standing here for long." I grabbed her arm, turned her, and walked her toward the front door. I heard Tiffani talking on her phone. "Time for you to leave."

"I'm not going anywhere until you hear what I've got to say." She stopped and spread her arms so I couldn't push her through the door. "You killed Reginald and made Judith's life so miserable that she called on Ed to help. Ed only wanted to make life easier for his sister. He's almost convinced her to sell Boulangerie. But Devon's decided he doesn't want to sell the bakery, so now Ed's upset, and Judith's upset. You've done nothing but throw everyone in this town into misery."

"That's not true." Something terrible had ticked this woman off. Had Ed said something?

"Now Ed's gone off, and I don't know where he is." She wailed. "It's all your fault."

Two policemen sneaked toward the front door. "Tiffani, let the policemen in, please."

Sobbing into a shredded tissue, the woman ignored me as the cops entered. At my elbow stood a young, buffed-out policeman. "What's going on here, Miss?" His nametag read *Yastrzemski*.

"I'm Sarah Murray, the manager of this bakery. This woman barged her way in and accused me of killing people."

The cop's partner, a squat, take-no-prisoners-type female, took the distraught woman aside. She sobbed, leaning against the counter, sputtering out her story.

Yastrzemski glanced at the two women, then back at me. "Do you know this woman?"

I shook my head. "Although from her ravings, it sounds like she is Ed Strange's wife, but no, I don't know her. Ed is Judith Bateau's brother."

"Who did she accuse you of murdering?" His dark, penetrating gaze scoured my face.

"Reginald Bateau. But she doesn't know what she's talking about."

"Even if she did, no one would take her seriously with those histrionics."

I thought a moment. It was better to be forthright in this instance. "Just so you know, I am the one who found Bateau's body."

His eyebrows rose, then settled down to their previous neutral expression. "And you've never met her before?"

"No. I met her husband a few months ago. He came in here impersonating a county building inspector and threatened to shut the bakery down." Uh-oh. I'd already said too much. But I guess they need to know this to do their job correctly.

"That seems kind of off-the-wall. Why would he do that?"

"It's only speculation, but maybe because they're related. My guess is that Reginald put Ed up to it because this place is—was—competition for Boulangerie." This was a small town. There seemed no need to go into who owns what business. Yastrzemski apparently already knew.

"And Judith is a bit high-maintenance." I was surprised that he voiced that observation. With a frown, he studied Ed's wife. "She must be leaning on her brother a bit much."

"Yes, my thought exactly."

The blond officer left the woman in a corner while she came over and conversed with Yastrzemski out of my hearing. Then she returned to Ed's wife and escorted her outside. They turned the corner and walked out of sight.

"There was no real crime here, right? I mean, she disturbed your peace..."

I put my hands up. "No, I'm not interested in pressing charges, Officer. I just want her gone, and she is. So thank you."

Yastrzemski smiled, tipped his index finger to his forehead in a salute, and walked out.

I gave a rueful grin to the barista standing wide-eyed behind the counter. "Thanks for calling the cops, Tiffani. Go home and put your feet up. You earned it."

O n the way to see Mark at Tom and Anna's, I stopped off to pick up Rusty. Before visiting, I wanted to walk and think through what happened today, just the two of us. Rusty didn't contribute much to the conversation, but he was a good listener. There wasn't anyone to talk to or see, so I felt like I was still safe from any more threats. I hoped the murderer saw my distance from the investigation.

Still, there were several threads of one story tickling my interest. Tickling was the operative word. There wasn't anything substantial enough to grab onto. After a few miles on Mumy Lane, I piled my rescue mutt into the Camry and headed over to Tom and Anna's.

Anna greeted me, as always, with a warm hug. She led me through the house to the back-screened patio. Mark was enthroned in a large wicker chair, shoulder in a sling, and his leg elevated. A nasty black eye accented the scratches from gravel on his cheek. Anna returned with a frosty glass of her homemade lemonade for me as I sat opposite my cousin. Anna found something else to do in another room.

"Are you here to make peace?" Mark took a long pull on his own lemonade.

"I thought we already had." I chewed my lip.

He cocked his head to one side in an endearing gesture he'd used since childhood. "Yeah, I guess so."

I snorted with exasperation. Sometimes he was so trying.

"Yeah, okay. For sure. We're blood, after all."

"We're more than blood, Mark. We're the accumulation of all the adventures we had as kids. Like the campouts in our backyard when your parents were out of town, milking cows, helping the moms with the harvest." I'd almost forgotten how we called Anna and Meg *the moms*. "We have so much history together that I'd hate to blow it all out of anger. Remember when your dad taught the three of us mutton busting?" Mutton busting is a rodeo event for children like bull riding. During the event, a sheep is held in a bull chute. A child is placed on the animal's back. The sheep is then released by opening the chute gate, allowing the animal to run freely into the arena space. Scores are had by holding on for eight seconds. Many adult bull riders swear they got their start mutton busting at six years old. It's fun for everyone, including the sheep, if you count bucking off a six-year-old as fun.

The sound of his laugh soothed the wounded place in my heart where he and Melody had existed. Melody was gone, but now, at least, I had Mark.

"Ha! She did better than I did." He slapped the side of the chair in delight with the memory. "Everybody was expecting me to go on and do rodeo. We fooled them. I didn't do rodeo, but you and she did."

That brought us to our separate memories of Melody. We sat in silence for a few moments until I asked, "What was your life like in Mexico?"

He took a deep breath and hid a smile. "It was hard work mostly. Planting, watering, spraying for bugs, harvesting, then hiring workers to come in and do the processing. That's tough because you need to hire people you can trust, yet it's a transient type of worker. You don't always get the same people coming through."

"What made you decide to come back?"

"I watched Jalo and Octavia. They had such happiness with their family, even though they didn't have anything. No car, no phone, no money. But they had each other and their kids, and sometimes his mother. I saw them every day. Some days, Octavia was a bit crabby. Maybe the kids got on her nerves, whatever the reason, Jalo not only put up with it but made her smile. Every. Time."

"They were rich with the love of their family." I thought about how it applied to the Murrays. We loved each other, but there were only three of us, not counting the Gibsons. As an only child, I was beginning to feel the weight of continuing the Murray/Gibson legacy.

He nodded, his long hair falling into his face. With his good hand, he swiped it behind an ear. "I grew to envy them. To want that for myself. One day it dawned on me. I had it. All I had to do is allow it. I had a family that would love me if I'd let them. Up till then, I hadn't allowed anyone to love me unless it served me or fulfilled some need I had at the moment." His eyes had a faraway look, back in Mexico watching Jalo and Octavia, I guessed. "Mom and Dad know this now. I told them last night. How I grew up over those weeks of watching that family. And how I began to miss my mother and father.

I'd already started the transition to legal crops. And invested in Jalo with a herd of goats. Then, when I heard about Melody, I knew I had to end my Mexican adventure and come back to Bishop."

The beauty and irony of his story made me sigh. I was happy for Jalo and Octavia and their brood. I was even happier at the model of family that it had exhibited to Mark. I wasn't sure he'd have made the revelations about his own family without their example.

I recognized the garage/kitchen door squeaks and the grocery bag thump on the counter. Tom bustled into the kitchen from the garage, home from his errands, carrying a bag of groceries. I stood with a smile as he sauntered out to the patio. Anna followed with a bottle of beer, handed it off to her husband, and returned to the kitchen. Tom settled into his favorite chair, a mate to the wicker one that Mark sat in. I sat back down on the sofa.

"I saw the oddest thing this morning." Tom took a swig from his beer and rolled the icy glass over his broad forehead. "I wouldn't be repeating this except for what's going on around here." He looked side to side, horror-movie style. I suppressed a grin as he continued. "I'd just left Von's Market downtown, and standing there in the middle of the parking lot was Judith Bateau and a young guy who was probably her kid. They were both arguing with a tall, skinny man. I mean, they were really arguing. I watched for a minute, thinking they might go to blows. The kid finally pulled his mom away, and they got into a car, then left. It was quite a scene."

I leaned forward. "When was this?"

He studied his watch. "Oh, I'd say ten o'clock this morning."

I stood to leave. "Thanks for that, Tom. I'm not sure

how it fits into this puzzle, but I appreciate you telling me. Now, it's time for Rusty and me to hit the road and leave you people to yourselves."

Chapter Fifty-Six

Dinner with Mom and Dad was light, a salad with slices of leftover tri-tip and French bread. After hearing Mark's story about Jalo and Octavia, I slowed down a bit and savored the moments with my parents. They listened to me and sought my opinion. I felt respected in a way I'd sorely missed with Blaine. Jake had the same qualities. When that thought clicked, something else changed in my heart. It would take some time to sort it out, but I sensed that I'd turned a corner.

Dad had some computer work to do after dinner, and I helped Mom with the dishes. I told her about my visit with Mark and the reason for his return. "All those years in the courtroom have honed my sense of honesty. Mark was telling the truth. I'm sure."

Mom sighed and draped the dish towel over the oven handle. "I trust you, kiddo. But I still worry about Tom and Anna. They are precious to me, and I'd hate to see them hurt—again."

"Me too. Trust isn't easily won back after so many hurts. I get your reluctance to believe in him."

My phone chimed a text from Wesley. *Got a SAR call out to Big Pine Canyon. May go all night into tomorrow. Will you check on my cats?*

I replied, *Of course, keep me posted if you need anything.* I was happy to hear he thought of Melody's two kitties, Ginger and Booboo, as his cats. He'd never been a cat person, but now that Melody was gone, he fell in love with the two furballs that she'd cherished so dearly.

Sure, thanks. Maybe a suicide, but not sure.

After dinner, I called Jake. His department emergency was well under control, and he was back to his usual schedule. He'd been texting me for a follow-up on what I knew about the investigation. I suspected he compared notes with Kelly McSorley at the sheriff's office. The two lawmen had developed a solid rapport. Kelly used Jake as a sounding board who offered experienced police practices. Jake picked Kelly's brain about local events surrounding the homicide to keep one step ahead of me.

Also, Mark's remarkable honesty with his family was bothering me. I believed him. The troublesome part was that I wasn't as honest as I should be. I held nothing back from Mom and Dad, but Jake was another matter. Yes, I wanted to protect him from the events of the past week. Distance precluded him from helping me. But the most cogent reason was I wanted to spare myself from being lectured, warned, or otherwise reprimanded. Mostly I merely expected it, even though Jake had only cautioned me twice. As I deliberated, I came to suspect most of my dread was a reaction to my ex-husband, Blaine. The relationship failure wasn't solely due to one person's actions. The breakdown occurred when one issue went wrong, and we didn't talk it over. One person tried to protect the other when the pair of us should have worked it through. I was guilty of holding back. At first, to protect Blaine, in the same way I was doing with Jake, then to protect myself from his temper or judgments. How could I expect anything different if I presented the same behavior to Jake?

And Jake was far away enough that I could easily get away with omissions. Omissions is another word for deception, and I didn't want to repeat the mistakes I'd made with Blaine. Jake and I were just beginning our relationship, and the deceptions I'd already committed bothered me.

I needed to update my expectations and take a long look at the man Jake Charters was. Could I share the rest of my life with him? Yes, I thought so.

I picked up my phone and tapped on his icon. "Jake? When will you be here next?"

"Funny you should call. I just submitted my request for three days consecutive to this weekend."

"You'll be here Friday?"

"No. I'll be there tomorrow, Wednesday, in the afternoon or evening."

"Oh, that's even better." I smiled into the phone. "I'd like to talk about our future, but I want to do it face-to-face."

"Okay." His tone said he wasn't sure how to take this news.

"There's nothing to worry about, Jake. We need to talk a few matters out. It will be good, I promise." I need to come clean.

In the guarded tone I'd heard from cops many times before, he signed off, promising to see me tomorrow.

Now I'd done it. He would worry.

Chapter Fifty-Seven

Wednesday morning dawned bright and hopeful. When I let Rusty outside, I felt the cool nip of autumn. The cottonwoods in the distance near the irrigation ditch were beginning to shed leaves. I shivered. Soon it would be harvest time, then Halloween. Then the holidays.

What would my holidays be like this year? Certainly, they had to be better than last year. Blaine had left for the entire month of December, allegedly to scout a movie location for a ski epic. But that had been only partially true. Lies and infidelity were not on my agenda for this year's festivities.

But today was glorious. The bright sun brought the stunning vista out our back door into stark relief against the azure sky. The air was clear and still. I stood, soaking up the scene, inhaling the scent of sagebrush.

In my bedroom, the phone trilled. Seven o'clock. It was early for a social call. My neck hair stood up.

When I answered, Anna whispered into the phone. "Sarah, can you come over? Now?"

"Sure, let me take a quick shower…"

She cut across my answer. "I need you now. The police are here, questioning Mark."

"I'll be right over."

I called Javier at Layers and told him I'd be late. Then I threw on a pair of jeans, T-shirt, and a sweatshirt, tucked my phone in a pocket, and trotted along the footpath behind the houses. We'd worn that path down as kids from our house to the Gibsons', and now it was overgrown. The parents used the road infrequently.

Anna answered the door. "Tom's working. I called but couldn't reach him." She led me into the patio room where two Bishop police officers stood facing a sleepy-headed Mark. From between them, Sergeant Foster snarled at me. "You're the proverbial bad penny, Sarah Murray."

Anna puffed out her chest. "She's as close to an attorney as we could get this early in the morning."

Foster ignored her and crossed his arms over his chest. "Okay. You want to be that way about it, we can go to the station for these questions."

"It makes more sense to stay here, doesn't it? I mean, is the PD set up for a wheelchair?" That was a stretch. Mark was walking with difficulty, but he hadn't needed the wheelchair the hospital sent him home with.

Foster's face flushed as he pulled out a pen and notebook from his breast pocket. The two officers shifted from one foot to another. I don't think they were any more thrilled to be there than I was.

"No? Well, aside from being an ADA violation, it would make your questioning much more difficult, don't you think?" I happened to know that BPD was retrofitted for disabled persons. The contractor who would be doing the Layers renovations had used the police department's as a reference. "So, we're staying here." I sat in Tom's chair next to Mark. "Ask your questions."

Over his notebook, Foster squinted at Mark. "When did you get into town?"

I held my hand up. "Wait a minute. You already asked him this a couple of days ago. His answers aren't going to change."

"This is routine, Sarah."

"It's Miz Murray to you."

His face flushed a deeper red. The two policemen on either side looked like they'd like to crawl away. "Okay, Mark, answer the question."

"Tuesday, at around eleven o'clock." He looked at me deferentially. "Miz Murray will attest to that."

"What time did you leave Layers?"

"About eleven fifteen or so." He shrugged.

"Where did you go when you left there?"

Mark's shoulders slumped with impatience. "I already told you. I had a buddy tow the broken down rental car to Wilkerson, where I was staying."

"And you're staying with your brother-in-law?"

Mark nodded. "I was at the time, yes. I was staying with Wesley Charters."

"Why are you here now?"

This seemed irrelevant to the line of questioning he'd been pursuing, but I didn't make a fuss.

Mark answered. "These are my parents. They were gone when I arrived and didn't know I was coming, so I didn't have a key. My mom's taking care of me."

"Sergeant Foster." I was getting tired of his bicep-flexing. "You already have all these answers. Why are you here asking again?"

Foster cocked his head toward Mark. "It seems his alibi is in the wind."

"What?" Mark sat up, as did I. "Wait. Pete's bow hunting in Mono County somewhere. You can't reach him because there's no cell reception up there."

"Convenient." Foster snapped his notebook shut. "How long will he be gone?"

Mark's good arm flew up in a helpless gesture. "I don't know. Ask his wife."

"I will. In the meantime..." He stopped, probably recalling the last time he told the injured Mark not to go anywhere. "I'm watching you."

Mark sighed with frustration as they left. He grimaced as he said, "I think he meant to arrest me."

I waited until the door shut behind them and Anna returned. "I think so too. But all he has is circumstantial evidence, and that's not good enough—usually."

Chapter Fifty-Eight

A t home, I took a quick shower and threw on my work clothes, khaki pants, and a nice polo shirt with the Layers logo on it. I hadn't heard from Wesley, so I assumed he was still in Big Pine Canyon. I hopped into my Camry and headed to Wilkerson to feed Ginger and Booboo.

When I drove up Wesley's driveway, dust was still settling around his RAV4. His screen door flapped open, so I walked up to the open door. "Wesley, it's me, Sarah."

He hollered to come in, and I found him in the kitchen. He'd just fed the kitties and flashed a tired smile at me. His hair was dusted with the gray dust from the glacier that formed the canyon, his hands and fingers were scratched from climbing and hoisting with rope. I feared the worst.

"You found your missing person?"

He nodded as he filled the kitties' water bowl. He placed it in their spot in the adjoining laundry room and straightened slowly as Booboo nudged his way to the bowl. "A recovery, I'm afraid."

"A suicide?"

He cocked his head sideways and answered. "It looks like it, but I don't know for sure. Someone said something about finding a note but..." He shrugged, not willing to speculate further.

"I'm sorry." Wesley always hated recoveries. It meant that search and rescue hadn't gotten to the person in time. Wesley was an optimist and always worked and prayed for the best outcome.

I offered to make him a pot of coffee. It was early enough that he might plan on going into his office at church. "That would be great." He dropped into a kitchen chair and rubbed his red-rimmed eyes.

"Have you eaten? I could make you a sandwich."

He waved it away. "I had a bunch of energy bars, and they filled me up for now. I'll drink some coffee with you, then take a shower and go to the office."

I sat across from him, two cups of steaming coffee between us. The brew was too hot to drink yet, so he began telling me about the incident. "The guy's wife called the sheriff to report her husband missing and said he'd left a note for her. The deputy went to the house and picked it up. He seemed to think it could be a suicide note. Apparently, his sister said he mentioned he and his nephew hiked up in Big Pine Canyon a while ago and really liked it. But no one was sure where he'd gotten to. The sheriff made the decision for us to respond, and we got the call out late afternoon. That's always a problem in those canyons. The shadows are tough. We searched the trails first and turned up nothing. The guy had left no car, which was odd."

I took a tentative sip, then took a drink. The coffee had cooled enough.

"It was full-on dark when one of the guys spotted a pair of glasses. They'd reflected off his flashlight…"

"Wait. Who was it?" Ed Strange wore glasses like that. "Do you know the victim's name, Wesley?"

He seemed surprised at my sudden interest. "Yes, his name was Edward Strange."

My heart thumped wildly in my ears. What could this mean?

I didn't know, but I was sure glad Jake would be here later today.

Chapter Fifty-Nine

Scrounging around in Wesley's fridge, I was able to come up with a breakfast of cheesy scrambled eggs and toast while he showered.

"Jake will be here this afternoon." Wesley smiled with a distinctly Charters lopsided grin. My heart grew another size to see the care these two men had for each other.

"We talked last night." I slid a plate of buttered toast on the table. "I'm looking forward to discussing the Bateau murder with him. He's got the experience to give me a fuller picture of how these things are done."

"I don't remember you ever being so inquisitive when we were kids. You've become a regular detective." He sat at the table, taking up a fork. "Tell me what you've got so far."

He chewed thoughtfully as I laid out what I'd uncovered. I practiced telling the entire truth, not leaving out what I thought he might not approve of. I concluded with the threatening notes. "Frankly, because of the threats, I've backed off the questions. I've been reluctant to be seen asking anyone anything. At first, I thought the warning was aimed at Rusty, but now I can't help but believe Mark's incident was caused by the murderer. His message is that no one is out of reach if I keep up my snooping. Honestly, I've been considering Ed Strange as a possible suspect. Only, I can't pin down his motive."

"Sarah, you take on too much. It isn't your responsibility to find out who killed Reginald."

"You're right, of course." I sighed, buying time while I found the words. "Foster pointed to me as a suspect. That scared me. It's already cost me months of work with kids enrolled in Better Off Baking. The county Office of Education shut me down until I'm exonerated. It could very well endanger my court job too."

"Sarah." He sighed with exasperation. "That job is your future. Putting it in jeopardy isn't wise. Now's the time for you to start working toward your own future."

I nodded. "I've got the job with the county rolling."

"Good. You've got Layers humming along. The money you're sending helps me considerably. The church salary isn't enough. I don't have another trade, so I was in danger of not being able to make the rent with this place. Layers' money helps. Now with Javier, it looks like Melody's and your good work will continue."

"I'm glad I'm able to help."

He nodded with as much enthusiasm as his fatigue would allow. "Just last week, I was at the bank to rearrange the church accounts and my personal finances, so the money goes where it's most needed."

Something tickled in my mind. "That's right. You said you were at the bank. What day?"

"Tuesday. The day Reginald was murdered."

"Do you remember the time?" Please remember.

"Yeah, it was around the time you found his body.

Larry and I saw the cop cars screaming down Main Street."

"Had you been in Larry's office for long? Together, I mean."

He polished off the last of his toast and swallowed. I heard the kitchen wall clock ticking. "I had an eleven o'clock meeting, and I wasn't late. So, from then until after the cops arrived, we were in a meeting."

Oh my. Wesley was with Larry Nixon at the time of the murder. That meant the two men could alibi each other. The bank cameras would verify their presence. I was happy to cross Wesley off the suspect list, although I never really felt he could be capable of such a grotesque murder. Larry Nixon, hmm. I didn't know him well enough to get a feel for him, but now that was irrelevant.

So back to Ed Strange. Did he commit suicide out of remorse for killing his brother-in-law? I wondered if we'd ever know.

What if he didn't do it?

Chapter Sixty

I got back to the bakery at eleven o'clock. There was only one viable suspect left on my mental list—Harlan Evers. Still, I thought it best to hold off any further sleuthing until the full picture of Ed Strange's death could be viewed. On the off chance that Ed wasn't the murderer, therefore the person who'd threatened me, I'd listen and learn for a while.

Libby had just shoved a tray of pain au chocolat croissants into a baking rack by the ovens. With Libby's light touch, they were becoming my favorites. Proofing three times for the maximum allowable rest made hers the lightest, most flavorful croissants I'd ever tasted. Bishop folks were also enjoying them. The usual flavors were pain au chocolat, plain, and cheese. All three types were routinely sold out by noon the day they were made. But as we approached fall, Libby had been experimenting with different flavors. Pumpkin pie, spiced apple, and sugar and cinnamon were in the works.

Marie was at the mixing station working on cake batter, and Charlie pulled out a tray of bagels. Layers was a well-oiled machine. But more than that, it was a creative place where each employee had something to offer—even Tiffani. She and Javier were the only ones who made the espresso machine operate the way it was supposed to. Charlie and I could struggle along and make the most basic drinks, but Tiffani did the fancy decorations that made customers "ooh."

Libby was at my elbow. "Hey, I've got an hour. You wanna go to lunch? I'll drive."

"Oh no, you don't." The thought of holding on for dear life on the back of her scooter threw us into fits of laughter. "The Academy Street Café?" At her nod, I said with as much authority as I could muster, "We walk."

A spring salad with a half chicken salad sandwich sat before me. I was hungry as I hadn't eaten at Wesley's. I'd made a rule about snacking at the bakery. Otherwise, I'd start gaining weight. I stabbed a baby lettuce leaf.

"How long are you going to let the Office of Education keep BOB out of business?"

My jaw must have dropped. She rushed to say, "I get why the schools don't want a murder suspect teaching their students how to cook." She put her hand up at my protest. "But you're not a murderer. You haven't been charged. As far as I know, they don't have any evidence against you at all, do they?"

I struggled to admit she was right.

"So, it was merely a matter of you being the person to call 911."

I chewed. She was right. There wasn't any evidence at all other than proximity. In his lack of other viable suspects, Foster had centered on me. Libby had fanned the stirrings of anger that I'd had from the time I'd first spoken to the sergeant.

"Maybe I should go to the police department and talk

to Frank." I was thinking out loud. She was right. Something should be done. I didn't want to wait around for evidence, if any, to implicate Ed Strange, thereby removing me from the PD's radar.

Libby twisted her mouth with distaste. "I'm not sure how much control he has over Foster. I mean, Foster's dad is the city manager. What about approaching it from the Ed perspective?"

"Like meet with the superintendent down at the county offices in Independence?"

Her full lips splayed out in an expression that said I needed educating. "No. Think local. What about the guidance counselor at the high school?"

I caught my breath. "I hadn't thought of applying pressure to the superintendent via the guidance counselors. But Harlan Evers doesn't much care for me."

She twisted her mouth into a funny pucker. "Maybe, but he does care about the kids."

I was quiet, thinking.

"I'll go with you if you want. He likes me." She sat up, pride straightening her spine. "He's the one who lobbied for me to go to continuation school rather than being expelled."

Maybe it would work. Maybe if he saw what a productive, responsible young lady Libby evolved into, maybe he'd put in a good word with the superintendent. Maybe we could get Better Off Baking running again and save a kid or two.

Then, in the back of my mind was the thought that he was the only one on my list who didn't have an alibi for Reginald's murder. He might've even had a motive.

Chapter Sixty-One

"Olivia Armstrong!" Harlan Evers' eyes shone at seeing Libby. He threw his hands up with delight as he strode across the office to hug her. She tucked herself into his embrace, and I marveled at this former juvenile delinquent who had such a positive effect on those around her.

His eyes hardened with suspicion when they fell on me. He pulled away, weighing her with a critical squint. "Libby? What's this?"

Libby didn't know that I'd met Evers, so she introduced him. I cut off his thin-lipped snarl. "Nice to meet you, Mister Evers. I've heard wonderful testimonials about how you believed in Libby when no one else did."

Still in the same posture, he made a grunting noise.

"Libby, since you know Mister Evers, why don't you tell him why we're here?"

Libby was up for the task. It sounded like she'd already organized her thoughts. "Mister Evers. What do you know about Better Off Baking?"

Taken aback, he regrouped in a hurry. "Let me see. It's a local program to help high-school-aged kids with behavioral issues learn workplace skills."

"You get an A." Libby was in form, loving the moment when she could prove herself worthy of convincing an adult the merits of a cooking program. "Does it work, you may ask." She held out her arms, welcoming speculation. Before he could comment, she went on. "Yes, it does. I'm living proof."

Evers's eyebrows rose. Then he caught himself falling under her spell and crossed his arms over his chest. "Explain."

Libby had definitely prepared for this. She'd even gotten a few statistics together to illustrate her point. She gave an overview of the program, then explained the selection process and how each student would fit into the neatly tailored community of Layers Bakery. While it was too early to look at recidivism statistics, Libby formed a cogent argument for BOB's resumption in the fall. We were ready. We had the money. We even had candidates to choose from. All we needed were a few final interviews, and we could get the program rolling again.

He held his hands up against Libby's onslaught. "Okay, I get it. You're a persuasive argument for success. What do you want from me?"

It was my turn. Libby took a half step back and leaned her head to me. "Sarah?"

"Mister Evers. I'm the manager of Layers Bakery. My cousin, Wesley Charters, owns it. I'm sure you heard about the recent murder of one of Bishop's leading citizens, Reginald Bateau. I was the unfortunate person who found his body. The police haven't found any viable suspects, so for mere proximity, I'm being scrutinized as a person of interest."

Evers glanced from me to Libby. "What does that have to do with…"

"I'm coming to that. Last week I got a visit from Victor Rogers from the Inyo County Office of Education. He told me that my BOB program permissions have been denied for this quarter due to my role in the local homicide."

Evers gave me a look of suspicious bewilderment. "And you want me to do what?"

Libby jumped in. "We want you to go to the superintendent and convince him that the program must continue. Sarah is not the murderer. If it would make your job easier, I can get a letter from the police department saying so." Police departments didn't do that, but I was probably the only one in the room who knew it.

"That won't be necessary, Lib." He sighed deeply. I worried he'd say no and tell her that I was a meddlesome fool. I worried for Libby's sake. She seemed to put so much stock in Harlan Evers' ethics.

"Okay. But no guarantees. I've always gotten along with the superintendent, and I'll see what I can do."

"Today?" Libby's face beamed with eager expectation.

Evers cracked a thin-lipped smile. "Yes, today. I live in Independence, so I'll drop by his office."

Libby pulled a BOB flyer out of her backpack. "You might need this."

I smiled at her foresight. She had this planned. Well, good for her. Thank God she was in my corner.

"Thanks for stopping by, Libby and Sarah." We were being dismissed. Surely, he had to prepare for the beginning of school days.

As I got to the door, I heard, "Uh, Sarah. Can I speak to you for a moment?"

"Libby, here are the car keys. I won't be long." She left with a satisfied smirk.

"Thank you for not telling the cops why you came to see me. They only wanted to know if I'd talked to you about the murder. I know you figured I was hiding something. I was... I am. I'm not prepared to give any more away than that, but I appreciate your respect."

He extended a hand, and I was happy to shake it.

In the car, Libby was ecstatic over her presentation. "I have a lot of faith in Mister Evers. He always does the right thing. If he hadn't stood by me, I would've been flushed down the toilet."

"He seems like a stand-up guy."

"What did he want?" That nosy little girl.

"Oh, it was about treating him with respect. He seems to think I know a secret about him."

Libby bent over with a huge guffawing laugh. I let her laugh until we got to Layers. In the parking lot, I parked and turned off the engine. She was still laughing.

"What's so funny?" I had to ask.

"Mister Evers' secret?" She settled down to a giggle. "His secret is that he's gay."

"That's not funny." I couldn't understand her reaction.

"No, but that he thinks it's a secret is funny. Everybody knows."

That's what Reginald had on him. I'd be willing to bet the person Evers was with at the time of the murder wants his identity to remain a secret, hence no alibi. "I see."

"The funniest thing is—everybody loves Mister Evers. No one would do anything to put him at risk, especially not to get him fired. He was the best thing about high school, as far as I'm concerned."

With another giggle, she got out of the car.

Chapter Sixty-Two

I sat in the patio room at Mom and Dad's, savoring the quiet. They were at a barbeque dinner with friends. After work, Rusty and I walked Mumy Lane. Dinner was a bowl of kibble for Rusty and a sandwich for me.

I thought about seeing Jake in mere hours. I'd last gotten a text from him outside of Sacramento four hours ago. With another two or three to go, he'd be here before six. I hoped. Traffic on this side of Sacramento wasn't usually problematic, but road construction was as unpredictable as winter weather. At higher elevations, which he had to travel, road repairs were done in the summer and fall seasons. During winter, roadwork was suspended. Winter temperatures and weather made roadwork impossible.

I had beer cooling in the fridge and sandwich makings if he didn't stop to eat.

I thought about what I wanted to say to him and how I would say it. I knew we'd have to get the regular business out of the way first and figured we'd be able to talk tonight. I felt an excitement and anticipation I hadn't allowed myself in months.

Engine noise came from the front driveway. He's here, I thought, jumping up and knocking Rusty off my lap with a jolt. I bent down and petted him, laughing at myself about saying, "I'm sorry" to a dog. Of course, Rusty was more than a dog, but I still laughed at myself. He padded alongside me to the front door.

An Inyo County sheriff's patrol vehicle sat tick-ticking in the driveway. I hid my disappointment and waved to the driver. Kelly McSorley opened the door and slid his bulk out of the driver's seat. He greeted me with a smile and gave me his usual greeting. "Hiya, kiddo. Jake's on his way. I just heard from him a half hour ago."

Jake's white SUV pulled up behind Kelly a moment later. Jake got out and stretched his back while opening the back door for Arco, his former partner. Rusty rushed past me to meet Arco in the driveway. They wrestled with tails wagging furiously. Both dogs whined and snorted their delight.

I walked past Kelly and reached for Jake. I wrapped my arms around him in what must have been a surprise because he squirmed until he figured out what I was doing. Then he wrapped his arms around me and whispered in my ear. "We'll talk soon."

"You look tired."

He shrugged. "I had to hold over, so I got about three hours of sleep."

"And a long drive on top of no sleep." My palm slid down his cheek. His stubble tickled my hand. He tipped his head as if this wasn't new for him to be so tired. And it wasn't. He often traveled after working a long shift with little or no sleep under his belt. I loved that he wanted to be here bad enough to give up sleep. But I worried about his lack of sleep while driving.

Unselfconsciously, we disentangled ourselves. Jake slung his pack over his shoulder and strode to Kelly. They grasped fists and clasped each other in a heart-to-heart bro hug.

"Come on in, you two. It's too hot to stand in the driveway."

Five minutes later, Jake had a cold, sweating bottle of beer in his hand. Kelly was in uniform on duty, so he got iced tea. We settled into chairs in the patio room. It was warm, but the fan moved air around to make it comfortable. This was one of my favorite rooms.

We caught up on family stuff, mostly Mark's incident and the police interview. Jake listened and made no judgments—at least out loud. We watched the dogs enjoy each other for a minute. Arco had gotten stiff during the long drive and relished the exercise. Rusty was young enough to give him a rousing welcome.

"Have you eaten?"

Jake nodded. "I stopped at that gas station at the Tioga Pass turnoff. Great food, by the way."

"The Whoa Nellie Deli at the gas station? Yes, great food." He'd eaten. Now, to check on Arco. Months ago, I'd changed dog food to the same brand as Arco's. "Has Arco eaten?" We had plenty on hand.

"I didn't want him to throw up over the mountain roads. So no." Jake smiled as I got the bowl from the cupboard we'd kept for Arco and filled it. I put it out in the yard and called him, although he seemed more interested in keeping up with the junior dog.

All chores had been attended to. It was time to get down to business.

Jake took the lead. "Kelly, what's been going on around here?"

Kelly leaned over his folded hands and began with a quick glance at Jake. "I filled you in on the body in Big Pine Canyon." They must have been in touch over the phone.

At Jake's nod, Kelly continued. "I got a search warrant for the victim's home today. The wife wasn't cooperative, so we had to do it the hard way." Kelly took a deep breath. A search warrant took time to write and find a judge to sign off on it. "We found boots with flour on them shoved under some clothes in the back of his closet. I'd be willing to bet when forensics results come back, they'll match the footprint found at the murder site."

He let that sink in. So Ed was the murderer. His suicide might be questionable.

Jake said what I was thinking. "It sounds like the only question now is, did Ed really kill himself? Or did he have help?"

"There are a few inconsistencies that our detective is concerned about. Like how did Ed Strange get there? There wasn't a car in the parking lot that is unaccounted for."

"Unaccounted for?" Jake's forehead furrowed. "You mean like backpackers' cars?"

"Right. Cars have to have permits so we can track hikers for their safety."

"Makes sense."

"Also, the wife has gone off the rails. My detective, Quentin Powers, knows the family. Kids went to the same school, that sort of thing. He said Ruthie has always been a mousy type, did what her husband told her to, never even got a ticket." He sat back into the chair. "Then, for her to go off like this is uncharacteristic."

"Nothing like knowing your constituency." Jake smiled at his buddy. "Go on."

"Powers said Ruthie has been babbling about Judith Bateau and how she's responsible for all this trouble."

Jake sat up. "Aren't Ed Strange and Judith Bateau brother and sister?"

"Yep. And it sounds like they've been battling about the business, Boulangerie. Ed wanted her to sell it, and Judith is dragging her feet."

"Has the crime scene been released yet?"

"As of this morning, it's still sealed up. Foster said he'd open it up later today or tomorrow when he makes an arrest."

"Arrest?" Jake and I echoed each other. Jake took my protest and ran with it. "Who's he going to arrest? Any ideas?"

Kelly shook his head and squinted at me. My cheeks had warmed with embarrassment. "Sure hope it's not Sarah."

Chapter Sixty-Three

S hocked, I dropped back into the chair's upholstery. "It can't be. There's no proof that I did it. I didn't do it."

"Let's not freak out about this yet." Jake's calm voice brought my blood pressure down a notch. "There's no way he can arrest you for murder. Like you said, he doesn't have any proof."

My stomach roiled with anxiety. "Besides, there are other strange incidents going on around here."

Kelly sipped his iced tea, then nodded. "I've been looking into Mark's accident. The more I investigate, the more I think it might not have been accidental."

"You mean it was intentional? Like somebody caused the jack to fail?" Jake swallowed the last of his beer. "Or maybe Mark set it up to happen for sympathy or attention."

The room was silent as we all considered the possibilities. I spoke up first. "I don't think Mark set it up. As much as I doubted him at first, I think he's back for good and has changed for the better."

Jake's lips thinned as he doubted my words. He reconsidered, then asked me, "Okay. I'll reevaluate my opinion of him based solely on your opinion. But I've got to ask. Why would somebody try to hurt him?"

I chewed my lip. "This is one of the reasons I want to talk to you tonight. There have been threats." I pulled out two notes from my pocket.

Stop asking questions that don't concern you, or you'll be sorry.

And,

No more questions. I warned you. You'll be sorry.

Kelly pulled out a copy of the note I'd given to Deputy Truelove. "This was found in Mark's pocket."

You're a victim of Sarah's meddling.

Jake was speechless. When he found the words, I saw betrayal in his eyes. "When were you going to tell me?"

"Tonight." Oh, the hurt in his tone tore my heart up.

"Why?"

I was reformulating the words I'd planned. Nothing seemed to make sense. I'd lied by not telling him the truth. I covered my mouth, worried I'd make matters worse.

Kelly spoke into his shoulder-mounted mic. I couldn't hear but didn't really care. He said, "I've gotta go. There's a verbal dispute between two women up on Bear Creek Drive."

Bear Creek? "Judith lives at 1589."

Kelly flashed a grim smile. "That's the address. What do you bet Ruthie's there causing a problem?"

Jake stood, rubbing his eyes. "I've gotta move my car so you can get out." Then to me, he said, "Let's talk tomorrow. I'm tired, and you're upset. I'll be at Wes's place."

Without allowing for my reply, he whistled for Arco, who bounded inside.

The next minute, I stood in the front doorway with Rusty, both of us wondering why everyone left so fast.

Bringing out through axis

Jake stood rubbing his eyes. "We're going to pull an all-nighter for this." "The... to this," he said, "let's a'll tomorrow. I'd rather, and you're in at. I'll be in. We're to be.

Although she up for my reply. I started to say.
She turned...

and before I could ask whether. "We have left so far"

Chapter Sixty-Four

Kelly called an hour later. "I want to make sure you're okay."

"Sure, considering I just dumped the best thing that ever happened to me down the tubes."

"He's upset, but he'll get over it. He's a reasonable guy, Sarah."

"Kelly, I as good as lied to him."

"Yeah, I was surprised you didn't tell him. You know, it's not my place to say anything to him."

"I know, Kelly. I'm not blaming you. This sits squarely on my shoulders. I wanted to protect him from worrying. He's so far away, he can't do anything."

Kelly snorted. "He's not a guy who needs to be protected, Sarah. You messed up this call."

"I know. I know." I did. "What happened with Judith?"

"Uh, I was going to call to tell you about this anyway."

My stomach flipped. How could this evening get any worse? "Go on."

"Judith Bateau and Ruth Strange were fighting. It wasn't physical, but they were out on the driveway of Judith's house, so the whole neighborhood heard them. It seems that Ruth thinks Reginald and Judith made Ed's life miserable. Ruth said her husband, Ed, tried to act as a mediator between Reginald and Judith. With Reginald's murder, Ed felt he'd failed so spectacularly—her word, not mine—that suicide was the only way to escape the shame. Judith had been drinking, so her filter was gone. Anyway, she said Ruth was a crackpot who drove her husband to suicide."

At least Ruthie wasn't blaming me. "Were you able to resolve their complaints?"

"Not a chance. I'm not a shrink." He cleared his throat. "But the one item they both agreed on was that you were to blame for all their troubles."

Darn. "Me?"

"I know. They both think that if you'd left this all alone, no one would've gotten their panties in a bunch. But I couldn't talk them out of it." He sighed the futility of a street cop who tried to reason with a drunk. Couldn't be done. "In the end, I told Ruth to leave and had Judith's son promise he'd stay with his drunk mother tonight."

I thanked Kelly for his call, grateful to have a friend like him. I was sure that any cop would've warned me after both women's accusations. But he was right. I'd botched up more than my relationship with Jake. I'd caused Mark's injuries and now maybe even Ed's suicide.

I had some serious soul-searching to do.

Chapter Sixty-Five

I'd never been much of a drinker. In college, I'd gotten drunk a few times but hated the hazy, logy feeling the next day. I felt much the same way the day after Kelly's call. I'd texted Jake, and his reply was, *Let's talk later.* I had no idea what later meant, today, tomorrow, ten years? I was in trouble, clearly.

I left Rusty at home with Mom, convinced she'd take better care of him. I'd worn my jeans and a blouse to work instead of my usual slacks and polo shirt. Tiffani was off, so I had the espresso machine duty, which made me cranky. Javier was my counter mate, so the morning wasn't all bad. Javier was managing the counter and the online pickup orders.

The front counter was trying, especially today. Impatient customers, not enough change in the register cashbox, in addition to a dustup between Charlie and Marie. I'd never heard Marie's voice over a whisper, so it caught my attention while digging out rolled coins from the office safe. I had no idea what the issue was, but I told them to resolve their problems and get back to work. I felt like I was channeling Reginald Bateau, the boss.

I cracked the wrapping off the quarter roll and filled the cash register. Another online order came in, but it could be filled quickly as there was no fancy coffee request. Javier bagged it up, and I had a free moment, so I volunteered to drop off the order outside. I tucked my phone in my pocket. A white 2020 Hyundai Sonata at the curb in front.

The car was at the curb, indeed. As I walked out the door of Layers, I leaned over to the passenger side. The door was wide open.

I smiled, handed the faceless driver the bag, and said, "Have a nice day."

Someone pushed me from behind. I felt myself tumbling. My fingers scrabbled for a hold on slippery vinyl as I fell headlong into the car. Another push from behind, and my whole body was inside.

Grunting with the struggle, I tried to push myself upright. I'd gotten my foot caught in a seatbelt strap. I heard yelling in the background. Was it the back seat? It sounded so nearby. No, it was Libby's voice yelling, "Stop!"

I sank into the seat as the car accelerated. Yanking my foot clear, my upper body tumbled into the floorboard. My rump lay half on the passenger seat. More yelling. From inside, a woman's voice.

Impatient hands grabbed my arm and tugged me toward an upright position. Another jerk and I wobbled vertical into the passenger seat. A man's voice was shouting now, firing orders to the other with a fierce tone. "Get that scarf around her face and neck. Tie her to the backrest."

A rayon scarf dropped over my eyes, and my fingers

flew up to stop it. I had to see what was going on. The scarf was sheer enough that I could see through it, thankfully. But it held me in place. Someone grabbed my hands, binding them together behind the headrest. Bangles clinked together as I placed the sound. Judith Bateau.

Tricep muscles stretched to the limit, I tried to find the ends of the scarf to pull it off. But I couldn't reach far enough. I sat, trying to quiet the thumping in my ears. I was sure these two kidnappers could hear my heart beating.

Who were they? I listened as the driver gave orders to Judith in the back seat. The driver was Devon Bateau. I could almost make sense out of him kidnapping me. He'd always felt I was responsible for his father's death. But Judith Bateau? Why would she be a party to this crime?

Judith's voice shook. "Devon, what are you doing?"

"What you should've done a long time ago. Dad needed this one to go away. So I—*we* are going to do it."

"No, Devon. I want no part of this."

"Too late, Mom." Devon hissed, "you're up to your elbows in this drama."

"No..." Judith's denial had a feeble tone that I'd never heard before.

"Kidnapping, Mom. That's a felony. We get rid of her now, and no one will know it was us."

"Are you kidding?" I thought a dose of reality might make them see the light of truth. "You heard my baker's voice at the curb. She saw you take me."

"Nobody believes that one. She's a party girl, been arrested and all."

Judith mewled, "No, Devon. No."

"It's her word against ours. We're the upstanding citizens, the backbone of Bishop society."

"Devon, no."

"Shut up, Mother."

They drove south on Highway 395—I could see that much—in silence as I thought of ways to convince them this was the wrong thing to do. Then it occurred to me that Devon was risking everything to shut me up. Why? What was he afraid I'd find out? Ed's boots had flour on them, but maybe he was working with Devon to put an end to his father's madness. It was worth a try.

"Devon, was it you who killed your father?"

"Nah. You're off base. Completely."

"Devon?" This came from the back seat. "Do you know who killed your dad?"

Devon tsked with disgust. "Of course I do. That's why I took care of him."

I repeated his admission as a question. "You took care of him?"

"We'll talk about it more when we get there."

Judith sniffled. "When we get where?"

I wondered too. We were headed south from Bishop. Their home was north. Devon slowed as we entered the town of Big Pine. My sense of dread was already in full blossom, but a new bud bloomed. A sudden turn to the right confirmed my suspicion. Big Pine Canyon.

I thought I'd try a different tactic. "Judith, we're headed to Big Pine Canyon. That's where Devon pushed Ed off a trail into the canyon below."

Devon remained calm. "You're pretty good at this, Sarah. You should've been a detective."

"You didn't, Devon. Tell me it's not true," Judith sputtered behind me. When he didn't answer, her anger took over. "I can't believe you killed him. Why?"

Devon shouted over her question. "Get over it, Mother. He's been nothing but trouble for you all your life. Just like my father."

I felt Judith's fingers quietly working to loosen the belt that held my wrists. "How did you know about Ed, though?" When they were loose, I kept my arms in place. Judith pulled the belt away slowly so Devon wouldn't see. She was keeping him talking to concentrate on his story and not us.

"You're so lame, Mom. Ed was the only person it could be. Ed hated Dad so much I'm amazed it took him so long to do it."

The road gained altitude, the engine straining at the climb. Judith's voice was a whimper. "But Ed was my brother. He only acted in my best interest."

"Ed was a loser. He never did one thing that didn't benefit him. He was after Dad's money. The joke was on him. Dad was broke. So are we, by the way."

"I know. He gambled it all away." The desolation in Judith's voice was unnerving. "Fantasy football was his passion. He tried to rein it in but never could for very long. It was his darkest secret. I didn't realize how bad it had gotten until that morning when he called."

"It wasn't a very well-kept secret. Ed knew, and so did I."

Judith's fingers loosened the scarf around my head but tucked it in place. "Did you ask Ed if he did it?"

"Sure. He denied it at first." Devon let out a hooting laugh. "But then I told him about the vocational school versus college debacle. It was so ironic that Dad was the fundraising king for local education, and his own son didn't go to college. That must have driven Dad bonkers. Ed thought Dad was a hypocrite but probably crazy too. Then Ed admitted stabbing him."

Judith moaned.

While Devon was admitting all this, it was time to get some answers. "Did Ed send me the threatening notes or you?"

He shrugged at the triviality of the question. "Must've been him. Wasn't me."

"How did you get Ed up here?" I saw the entrance sign to the Inyo National Forest, *Big Pine Creek Trailhead*. We'd passed the road to the campgrounds, so any chance to call out for help was gone. I figured as long as he was talking, we were safe, even if I asked presumptuous questions.

I wondered how Judith fit into all this. She clearly didn't know what her son had done. And bless her, she was risking his wrath to free me. Now, what I would do with the freedom was a good question. I'd have to be able to think on the fly.

"Ed? He was always up for nephew time. He knew Dad had messed up his sister's life and was about to do the same to me." He flipped on a blinker. I wondered who'd see it. "I think he was jealous of Dad. The opportunities he'd blown. And Ed couldn't have kids, you know."

Murder cannot be rationalized—ever. But a little ping of sympathy went off in me. How resentful Ed must have felt about not being able to have his own sons and daughters? Judith was sniffling, crying over the tragedy that was her family.

I kept talking. "Did Ed tell you about the decorations he..."

With a bellow of laughter, Devon slammed the heel of his hand into the steering wheel. "He told me. He said the icing was sitting there on the table. He did it for like, a joke. Dad always wanted everyone to look to him like he was the center of the universe. Ed thought it was funny. So did I."

Still chuckling, he pulled up to a stop. "Mom, you stay here. I don't trust you not to interfere." The scarf slipped, but Devon hadn't noticed. I saw enough to know we'd parked at the edge of an earthen escarpment. A breathtaking canyon lay beyond. Was this where Ed was pushed?

Judith grunted through her tears. Devon got out, rounded the front of the car, and stepped up to open the passenger door. As soon as I heard it click open, I pushed the door with all my strength. The scarf fell and draped around my shoulders; the belt was history. But my arms had gone numb, and my strength wasn't what it usually was. Devon stumbled backward and lost his balance. I bolted from the passenger seat and sprinted off to where I guessed the campgrounds were.

Devon scrambled to his feet and was after me. I heard his shoes pounding the ground behind me. Then, when I'd run halfway across the lot, he grabbed my hair and hauled me around to face him. His face was red, his temple pulsating, and sweat dripped off his nose.

He started to say something, but I yelled for help. I had no idea how far away campers were, but what did I have to lose?

Devon clamped his hand over my mouth and dragged me back past the car. Judith had opened the back door and reached out as her son pulled me by. It was a feeble attempt at stopping her son from causing another murder. Past the car, to the edge of the lot, the level surface dropped off dramatically. I tried not to look, but a quick glance told me the bottom was one hundred feet below. A hawk screeched from above.

"I'm tired of you."

I caught his arm and swung a fist at his chin. Letting go of my hair, he ducked. I'd already lifted my knee to smack him in the groin, so I was off balance when he righted himself and pushed me off the edge of the escarpment.

I fell, knees scraping against the glacier-cut rock. A scrawny shrub grew out of the dirt, and I grabbed it. It came away in my hand, but I reached for another a foot away. This one was rooted more substantially and slowed my drop enough to dig my sneaker toe into the dirt. I'd stopped the fall. But beneath me was a hundred feet of cliff. I couldn't see the bottom of the trees. I looked up. No Devon, but no car sounds either. I wasn't sure I'd hear them anyway.

Small rocks tumbled past me. I froze. If I moved, the bush could give way. My sneakers didn't have enough purchase to support me. I was stuck. I could shout for help, but who would hear me? I was miles from the John Muir Wilderness, which was just that—wilderness. Campers might not hear.

I was alone. Hanging from the side of a cliff, and no one knew I was here. Devon must've taken Judith with him when he left. He wouldn't leave her behind. Still, I called out. "Judith! Are you there, Judith? Help me!"

I hung on. The sun tipped over noon, and I felt the burn on my shoulders through my blouse. My forearms turned pink, then red. I called out again. Projecting how long I could remain here, desperation crept into my heart. How long? How long before I fell? I'd never survive the drop, much less the landing.

I felt as good as dead, the mountain sun beat down

on me. Sunburned and thirsty, my hand cramped from holding on. Ever so slightly, I shifted my body and grabbed the bush with my other hand. Pebbles and dirt dislodged and skittered down past me. Down. I never heard them land.

My regrets came to mind. All the possibilities I let slip through my fingers. Jake, especially. What a fool I was to put him off. He was the man I'd always dreamed about. He possessed all the qualities I wanted in a life partner. And I pushed him away. For no good reason. I heard my own voice call out his name, "Jake."

Now, we'd never have a future. We'd never have children, which I realized I'd desperately wanted.

Whoever called you Sensible Sarah, anyway?

Chapter Sixty-Six

Hours, or it could've been minutes later, I came to. The misty fog cleared from my brain, and my precarious position dawned. My hand cramped closed around the bush, but my toe had moved away from the tenuous purchase.

A big bird cawed in the chasm behind me. Noise. I heard noise. Campers? Hiker? A dog barking.

Barking furiously. He sounded anxious. Like someone made him angry.

As the sound grew closer, I recognized that bark. I'd heard him distressed like that before. Arco, who'd tried to save Melody. Arco. And Arco wouldn't be here without Jake.

"Jake." It came out in a whisper.

I was hot. I wanted a nice glass of ice-water. It was so hot.

"Sarah?"

Was I dreaming, or was that Jake's voice? Arco's bark cut through my nightmare. He sounded even more frantic, the sound growing nearer. Then Wesley and Kelly called for me. I opened my eyes, the glare of the sun behind me. I saw two of Kelly. I must call to him; he can't see me. Arco's dark snout peeked over the edge, then dropped back. I expected he'd sat in the I-found-it stay. For Jake.

"Kelly." A mere whisper through chapped lips. But I tried once more. "Kelly."

Then I heard them. Kelly, Arco, Wesley, and Jake. Kelly yelled at the others, and I heard them hollering back.

A rope dropped near my free hand. "Sarah, take hold of the rope."

I grabbed it with all my muscle and held on.

"I'm coming to get you, Sarah. Hold on." Wesley's voice was the practiced calm of a search and rescue worker who moonlighted as a preacher. It was music to me.

"Arco? Is Jake there?"

"Sarah, hold on." Wesley eased over the lip, skipped, and glided down to where I waited. I can't really say how this process went. I closed my eyes so I wouldn't know if I was hallucinating or not. I wanted Wesley to be there.

And he was. He called to me mere inches from my ear. "Sarah, wake up. We're here to bring you home."

I tried to smile, but my lips split. I felt a rope under my arms and heard the snick of a clamp closing. "Come on, Sarah," Wesley whispered in my ear. "We're in this together, and I need your help. Walk up with me."

The rope lifted us both. I stood on my toes, with my weight on the rope that encircled me. "Sarah, let's go."

It seemed hours to get up. One foot in front of the other. Then, finally, at the edge, arms caught me. Someone released the rope, and the arms tightened. He let me down to the ground, where I rested in his lap. I smelled the masculine scent of sweat and shampoo. Jake.

Jake.

He tipped a water bottle to my bleeding lips, and I drank. He pulled it away from me for a moment and held me tightly, saying my name over and over. He dampened a rag and mopped my face. Then a little more water.

I felt like I'd been swimming underwater and moving toward the surface. When I heard the siren in the distance, I knew it wasn't a dream. This was real.

Jake was here. I was on solid ground and not going to die.

Thank God.

"Jake, I've got to tell you…"

He shushed me. "We will talk later, my sweet, sensible Sarah. You can count on that. But right now, save your strength."

Kelly bent over Jake's shoulder and said, "Hiya, kiddo. Just hanging around waiting for us, were ya?"

I laughed. And laughed. And kept laughing until the ambulance drove up. Wesley must have thought I was hysterical. I guess I was.

Chapter Sixty-Seven

Later that evening, I awoke in a hospital bed. Jake stood on one side with Mom and Dad on the other. An IV bag on an aluminum rack hovered over my bed, the long tube dripping saline and fluid into my dehydrated body. I lifted my hand to say hi to everyone, then had to drop it. Jake leaned in and clasped it.

I was still weak. But the disorientation had faded. I knew where I was, who was with me, and what had happened.

Someone said Kelly's name, and he appeared in the doorway. He gave me a big goofy grin like when he'd won a spot on the high school junior varsity football team. He was as safe as a huge teddy bear, and I was lucky to call him my friend.

Jake scraped a chair across the linoleum and placed it opposite my parents. He took my hand again and held it tight. "You up for some questions?"

I hoisted myself to one elbow, then dropped back onto the pillows with my eyes closed. I was so tired. But there was business to be finished up. "Sure."

"Are you sure, Sarah?" Mom's voice sounded so anxious. Her brows drew together in her worried-as-heck look.

"I'm just tired, Mom." I opened my eyes and looked around the room. These people were my most beloved family. I wanted them to know the truth. I glanced up at Kelly, who stood with a notepad in hand. "Shoot."

"Start with how you got into Judith's car."

"Good question. No way would I've gotten into her car, especially with Devon driving. I got pushed."

Mom fired Dad a look that said *I told you so*. I smiled at them, then continued. "I was taking an online order to the car. I leaned in—the door was open—to give it to the driver, and someone pushed me inside. It must've been Judith because Devon was at the wheel. It took me a few seconds to figure that out."

"What happened next?" Kelly's pencil was poised to take the details.

"Devon told Judith to tie me up with her scarf and a belt on my wrists. Judith sounded kind of reluctant. I'm not sure she knew what Devon had in mind."

"Did either of them say anything?"

"Oh yes. Plenty. Devon figured out that Ed killed his father. He got Ed to admit it to him. His reasoning was that Reginald had ruined his sister's life and was going to do the same to Devon's." I explained about the vocational school versus college dispute. "Ed even told Devon about the icing. He said he noticed it after he stabbed Reginald. It was lying there on the table, and he thought it ironic how Reginald always had to be the center of attention. It didn't take long, so he added decorations on him."

Sighs of revulsion circulated in the room. Even Jake, who'd seen much in his career, shook his head. The sheriff's detective, Quentin Powers, entered the room, standing quietly by Kelly.

"Devon said he'd conned Ed into a hike up Big Pine Canyon. Then he pushed his uncle off the cliff for killing his father."

Dad sat up; his mouth twisted in a perplexed expression. "But didn't you say Devon told you Ed had got to Reginald before he did? He admitted he would've killed Reginald. Now Devon killed Ed for killing Reginald? That doesn't make any sense."

"No, it doesn't, does it? I think Devon was removing all the obstacles to his and his mother's happiness—Reginald and Ed." I took a sip of electrolyte-packed water. "Now the sheriff's office has to find Devon and Judith."

Kelly flipped his notebook closed and shoved the pencil in his breast pocket. "Already done, kiddo."

I nodded my gratification. "Now. Will you tell me your side of this adventure?"

Kelly smiled, pleased to repeat such an important report. "Libby called me directly. She came out front to complain about some employees in the back and saw you get pushed into the car. She copied the license plate down, so Javier had it for us. I was off duty at home in Big Pine. Libby couldn't tell which way the car was headed, so I hopped in my unit and headed northbound on Highway 395 to Bishop, on a hunch. I called Jake on the way and picked him up in Wilkerson. Coming out from there, we spotted the white Hyundai on Gerkin Road, you know, the road that parallels 395 for a ways? Devon had taken some back roads. We turned around and followed him at a distance. When he turned at Big Pine Canyon Road, we followed. We lost him on Glacier Lodge Road, but that's a dead end, so we figured we'd be able to catch him. Even so, he hid in one of the small parking lots off the road. We sent for more boots on the ground. Jake got the phone company to track your phone —we found it in your pocket—until the signal was lost. It took us a couple of hours to search all the lots. We were about to start all over at the beginning when we heard you call for Jake. Then Arco went nuts."

"Thank God for that." I sighed, trying not to think what would've happened if I hadn't called out. I'd still be there. "Did you find Devon and Judith?"

Quentin stepped forward. "We did. Foster from the PD found them sneaking into town on Poleta Road. We're holding both of them for kidnapping at the moment but will up the charges when we get all the questions answered. I'll be interviewing them after we get your statement. Glad to see you're on the mend, miss." Quentin nodded, turned, and left after a brief whisper to Kelly.

It turns out trouble didn't arrive in Bishop from where I had expected.

Chapter Sixty-Eight

T hat Saturday, the first annual Fall Colors Festival opened with a barbecued hamburger and hot dog lunch sponsored by the Bishop Lions Club at City Park. The afternoon was warm, but an autumn crispness freshened the air. Families in shorts and tank tops meandered the park, grabbing freebies from utility companies, snacking at the food trucks, and enjoying the permanent playground equipment. Many local nature groups were represented. Tom and Anna hauled in a calf and a pair of goats for kids to touch. Mono County Sheriff's Department provided their mounted patrol. Horses are always a draw but especially these specifically trained equines. A local hawking club presented exhibits of their predatory birds, the Eastern Sierra Audubon Club offered brochures on watching wild birds, fishing and hunting guides did the same, along with sage advice. All the sporting goods stores had tables and giveaways. Most of the area pack outfits had tables touting rides of various types. The busiest table was that of a fishing guide who offered a leaf peepers tour through Inyo and Mono Counties.

Libby's friend, Layers's marketing maven, had put out some spectacular advertisements online and posters around town. She even sent mailers to cities up and down Highway 395. There were so many cars that the police department needed help directing traffic from the highway patrol. City Park is on Bishop's Main Street, which is also Highway 395. The overflow parking was already filled at eleven o'clock, the opening time.

Fall Colors Festival appeared to be the event of the season, second to Mule Days. Everything ran smoothly, thanks to the chamber. Paula was as good as her word. When I had asked for power for vendors, she arranged with Southern California Edison to bring in extra generators. I heard no complaints, not even about the Porta Potties, which amazed me. The sanitary facilities were set up well ahead of time in the back of the park, away from the food concessions.

Event hiccups were minimal, including finding the parents of a lost toddler. I held the crying boy until his anguished mother found us at the information booth. Still, I was exhausted from the planning and preparation of this event. If it will be done next year, I kept notes on points that needed special attention or improvement. The chamber might not ask me back next year, so I had the notes to pass on to the new organizer. If they did, I wouldn't have to start from scratch. Still feeling residual fatigue from the Big Pine Canyon adventure, I found a picnic bench and sat. A noisy, honking flock of Canada geese flew over in their migratory journey south, joyously announcing autumn.

The afternoon sun cast dappled light on the manicured lawn. The day was warm but not too hot. After a short rest, I visited each vendor, making sure they had what they needed from the planning team. It was sometime right before three o'clock when Marie tugged at my shirt. "Sarah? Can you come over to the gazebo? You should see this."

I glanced at my phone—one more hour to go. I hoped Marie didn't have unwelcome news. Judging from the exuberantly expectant look on her face, she didn't. I was content to follow her. The gazebo was a substantial building that sat on the pond in the middle of the park. The Bishop Community Band hosted summertime concerts every week, but today, a crowd packed the gazebo to the railings.

Marie held on to the tail of my polo shirt and dragged me through the mass of people until we got to the center. People dropped back to make a six-by-six-foot circle into which stepped Libby and Cameron holding hands. Libby wore a vintage calf-length ivory satin sleeveless dress, the bodice trimmed in lace. A sprig of gerbera daisies pinned back the long side of her hair. Black booties complimented her outfit. She even wore mascara. Cameron was in jeans, as always, but these were new, a dark wash that hadn't yet seen sagebrush. Wearing a western cut shirt, with a brown suede vest and his Stetson, he looked a fine strapping version of a dressed-up cowboy.

When I noticed Wesley standing behind them, I figured out what was happening. I couldn't hide the shock from my voice as I faced Libby. "You're getting married."

Libby took a step toward me, her face glowing with happiness. "Yes, and you are the maid of honor." Into my hand, Marie shoved a small bouquet of greenery, privet berries, and grasses tied with raffia.

"But..."

Libby cut across me. "No buts, Sarah. Cam and I are getting married. I'd like you to share in our special day." Her forehead wrinkled with her plea. "Please."

I had misgivings. She—they—were both so young. I glanced around for Frank, sure he'd take a dim view of the proceedings. Finally, I spotted him standing next to Wesley. He winked at me, smiling, and whispered into Wesley's ear. They both chuckled.

If Cameron's dad was okay with this, who was I to protest? I had reservations for several reasons but kept them to myself as I accepted the bouquet from Marie. "I'm not dressed for this, you know." My polo shirt had the Layers logo atop the breast. And my chinos were hardly wedding togs.

Libby snorted with relief and took my arm. She positioned me next to her, facing Wesley. Cameron stood beside her, and Frank flanked his son. Still in shock, I missed much of Wesley's sermon. When it came time for their vows, Libby handed me her bouquet. She faced her husband-to-be and held his hands in hers.

"Cameron, I take you to be my one true love, my partner in life, and my best friend. I vow to comfort, encourage, and inspire you for the rest of our lives. I will forever be there to laugh with you, to lift you up when you are tired or down, and to love you unconditionally through all the adventures of our life together. You are my happiness, my love, my everything. I love you forever."

I couldn't help myself. I cried. They were tears of delight that Libby had found the happiness she so richly deserved, tempered with the concern for all the bumps in the road these two would have to endure. I had no doubt that they loved each other. But marriage is a day-in and day-out proposition. There was more to it than love.

Then it was Cameron's turn.

"Libby, the moment I met you, I knew I was in trouble." The crowd laughed. "I knew I couldn't live without you. You brought color to my black-and-white life. You have shown me what it means to be a genuine person. I am constantly amazed at your wisdom and kindness. I'm so anxious to begin our lives together. I promise to be there to share in your joys and sorrows, your dreams, and accomplishments. I want to celebrate with you and solve problems together. I promise to be the guy you and our future family can always depend on. I promise to be faithful to you, to love you, and be thankful every day that you came into my life. How lucky I am to be marrying my best friend. Libby, I love you."

After the *I dos,* rings were exchanged, and Wesley pronounced them husband and wife. The pair kissed, and Wesley introduced them to the crowd. "Everyone, please meet Mister and Missus Cameron Scherwin." The crowd whooped and hollered their congratulations. I stood back, focusing all my attention on Libby.

Wesley called for quiet and made an announcement. "Ladies and gentlemen, please celebrate with Libby and Cameron by enjoying a wedding cake…" He leaned over as Libby whispered in his ear. Then he straightened and continued, "…made by the bride. A salted caramel with vanilla sponge cake." Chuckles rippled through the group. "It will be served at the picnic benches over there." He pointed to where Marie and Charlie cut pieces of the cake, waiting for the crowd.

The crowd split, half going for the cake, the other half

mingling with the newly wedded couple. I hung back, hoping to catch a moment with Libby. I watched Frank with his son and was grateful for the evolution of their relationship. They'd come a long way from the uncooperative teenager and tyrannical father I'd first met.

Then Libby's hand was on my arm. "Sarah."

I whirled to face her. "Why didn't you tell me?"

"I knew you'd try to talk me out of it."

"I won't deny it."

"I'm sorry. I hated to go behind your back, but this is what I want. It's what we both want."

"I'm overjoyed to see you both so happy. You deserve it." The deed was done. She didn't need anyone chipping away at her about the possibility of mistakes. I really was pleased for her. Plenty of couples who married young make it for the long haul. Who was I to tell her otherwise?

"Have you thought about school?"

"Yeah. We have a plan for that. It's too late to get into Cal Poly for this semester, so I'm going to stay here at Cerro Coso Community College. I'm already registered. I plan on working at Layers until I move to San Luis Obispo to be with Cam. He's still going to school there."

I touched her shoulder. "I'm glad you're continuing your education—both of you. You have a gift, Libby. Melody realized it."

Libby's eyes grew dreamy. "I wish she was here. I miss her every day."

"Oh, she knows. She's watching you from heaven, and she is so proud of the young woman you've become." I smiled with the certainty of my statement.

Libby hugged me, a beat longer than I expected, but I held her tight.

"Lib, let's go get some cake." Cam hollered. I let go and shooed her away.

When Jake touched my shoulder a minute later, I fell into his arms, happy and exhausted.

Chapter Sixty-Nine

The festival was over, pronounced an inspiring success by the chamber and all who participated. Tom and Anna told me they booked almost a dozen pack trips for hikers and hunters in the coming weeks. I hoped all the vendors had done as well.

The next morning and early afternoon were taken up with cleanup matters: making sure borrowed tables and chairs were returned, generators picked up, the Porta Potties retrieved. The city public works department had fulfilled its commitment as there was no litter to pick up, no food to put away, or garbage to be emptied.

Late in the afternoon that day after the festival, Jake and I sat in the patio room at Mom and Dad's house. The sofa was comfortable, and I stretched out on it while Jake pulled up a chair opposite me. Mom had handed us each a glass of iced tea. Appearing reluctant to leave, she toyed with her apron strings.

"Sarah, I have to say something. It won't take long." I sat up. This sounded important.

Jake started to stand, but Mom protested. "No, Jake.

No need for you to leave." She faced me like a child caught taking candy from a bowl. "Sarah, remember when I said I trusted your judgment about Mark." She didn't wait for my acknowledgment. Her words rushed together. "Well, I didn't, really. And I didn't until I saw the proof of what you already knew." Her smile said she regretted dismissing my well-placed trust. "You were right. There was no need to protect the Gibsons from their own son." She began untying the knot at the end of her apron strings. "That's it. That's what I wanted to say. You were right." She turned, saying, "Now I'll leave you two alone." I heard a relieved sigh as she left.

I'd always respected my mother and savored her wisdom. This moment was no exception. Her words had more of an impact on me than she would've expected. I'd fallen into the same trap when I tried to protect Jake from my troubles when he was so far away. Her admission cut to my heart.

"She's a wise woman, your mother." Jake smiled.

"More than you know." I turned to face him. "There are things that I need to say to you, Jake Charters."

He nodded. "Me too. I guess it's time we discussed what's happened in the past few weeks as well as our future." He stopped suddenly and squinted at me. "Are you ready for this?"

"Very."

"Okay. I'll start. I guess we both learned lessons. I cannot keep you safe the way I'd like to. I can't build a wall around you so you don't get hurt. But besides being unrealistic, it's also the opposite of what you need. You need the freedom to make your own decisions. You're a responsible, independent woman who I respect beyond words. I'll always be there to give advice should you seek it, but you're an adult too."

"Thank you. I appreciate it." I touched his hand, and he smiled.

"My turn. I failed to account for the loss of your precious wife. It must've been hell not being able to save her when that's what you've dedicated your life to doing." I gave him a rueful smile. "I realize now you were trying to keep me safe."

He nodded thoughtfully. "But you're not Kristin. You're different, and I respect that. No, I love that. You'll get no more orders from me."

"You never ordered me. At least I didn't hear it that way, even if you meant it."

We both laughed softly.

I took a sip of the tea and cleared my throat. "When I was hanging from that bush, I had a flash of panic when I thought I'd never get to tell you how much I've grown to love you, Jake Charters." I savored his gentle smile. I continued. "With love comes the responsibility to tell you the truth. I don't need to protect you from worrisome matters in my life. You're a big boy, a policeman, for crying out loud. What was I thinking?"

"Yeah, what were you thinking?"

"I was thinking that I didn't want to push you away. I'd failed miserably with Blaine and worried that I'd make the same mistakes with you. But I shouldn't have worried. You and Blaine are entirely different people. I can be honest with you. There is trust in my vocabulary again. It doesn't matter what happened before. What matters is the lying and omissions—for whatever reasons —stop. Now."

Jake held me for a long time. I fell asleep and awoke later in my bed, Rusty snoring softly in his bed nearby. I rolled over and closed my eyes with hope in my future for the first time in a long time.

Chapter Seventy

The next morning, Jake showed up on the doorstep at the McLaren house. The crystalline sky behind him was so blue it could've shattered. A light breeze rustled elm leaves around the porch. With a ball cap in his hand and Arco beside him, Jake rested his weight on one foot, then the other. "Care to go for a drive today? I'd like to show you something."

My original plan was to lounge around after Saturday's festival. I was tired from all the planning and activity, but his invitation looked too tempting. "Rusty too?"

His smile broadened. "Of course."

Once in his SUV, we headed north on Highway 395. He must have known it before I did; I needed a break and a change of scenery. Climbing Sherwin Grade with an average gradient of almost six percent, the elevation jumped from just over four thousand feet in Bishop to almost sixty-five hundred feet at Tom's Place. Popping my ears was a full-time job.

As we passed the turnoff for Mammoth Lakes, I glanced at Jake. His sly grin told me he had something special planned. It wouldn't be lunch in Mammoth, though. Nor June Lake, another year-round resort. Both Mammoth and June Lake are primarily ski areas but have summer convenience amenities available to campers, hikers, fishermen, and other tourists. Many of the restaurants were excellent. I thought he'd planned lunch out of town.

Up ahead was Lee Vining, known as the gateway to Tioga Pass, which bisected Yosemite National Park. "You must have grabbed one of those leaf peepers' brochures at the festival yesterday."

"Nope. I saw this when I came over. I've been planning it since then. When we get to the overlook, I think you'll be amazed."

Rusty and Arco snored in the back seat. "How's Arco doing with retirement?"

He shook his head. "He's confused. When I go to the car for work, he wants to go with me. He doesn't understand the concept of retirement."

Arco's furry flank rose and settled with the even breaths of a deep sleep. A small snore escaped. I said, "He may not ever get used to it. Too bad he can't be repurposed like horses from the track. Sometimes they can be retrained to be jumpers and show horses."

"Hmm," his gaze became a stare as he pondered the idea. "Good idea. Maybe we can do something with him. It seems a shame to let all that drive and training go to waste. He's healthy enough to have another assignment. We just have to figure it out. Both his parents lived into their teens."

I laughed. "Right, because otherwise, he's merely going to be Rusty's playmate." I stopped, thinking how presumptuous that sounded. Jake lived three hundred and fifty miles from me, over a major mountain range.

While we were committed to each other, we hadn't discussed our futures. "I'm sorry. I didn't mean…"

He tipped his head in a gesture so like Wesley. "I know. We should start hashing out how we're going to make this thing between us work." Mono Lake was like glass. It disappeared behind us as we climbed higher. At Conway Summit, he turned left at Virginia Lakes Drive. This led to a campground, as far as I knew. But another left, and we left the tarmac and rumbled onto a dirt fire road. Bumping over gravel and rocks woke up the boys. Rusty sat up, sure he was going to chase balls soon. Driving slowly, we paralleled the highway for a way.

"Right." I thought about how I'd dreamed to build a life in my beloved hometown of Bishop. With my parents and other family close by. I couldn't see myself moving to another town, even Petaluma. While I'd never been there, Jake spoke of it so positively. Could I start over? Whether I wanted to move or not, the bottom line is that I wanted to be with Jake.

Jake began. "I want you to know that I have similar concerns to yours. You want—no, need—to be near your family. So do I. My dad is still in Petaluma and is established there. He has friends, golf partners, and a little bit of a social life. He's seventy and healthy, but he's slowing down. I have to be near him."

"In summary, we both have ties to where we live, including the area and family." I turned to him. "Sounds like an impasse has been reached."

"Not necessarily." Again, that tip of the head. "I may have something promising in the works, but it's too early to tell."

What? "Too early to tell me? Shouldn't you be sharing this with me? Why would you tell me half of this?" Excitement rose inside me, and speculation about what he was planning.

"To keep you interested." He laughed. "Seriously, I know you're not going shopping for a husband. But I'm sworn to secrecy about the details." He pulled the SUV to a stop. "It's time for your surprise." He lifted a hand toward the windshield.

I looked out, and my breath caught. The panoramic view of the vast meadow below Virginia Lakes sat tucked behind the rolling hills we'd just driven through, with the Sierra Nevada Mountain Range as its backdrop. Snow still capped the highest peaks. Below, a carpet of multi-colored Aspen trees draped the hills. Yellow leaves at the higher elevation merged into orange, red, and brown at the base of the rise. A strip of vibrantly green Aspens in the middle hadn't gotten the memo about the shorter days. On the mountains above, a swath of Jeffrey and sugar pines contrasted the vivid fall deciduous trees.

I blew out an unrestrained sigh. Although I had only driven past here on infrequent visits to Reno relatives, I'd never seen such a display. This spectacular show was the perfect conclusion to yesterday.

"I knew you'd love this." Jake curled his arm around my shoulders and pulled me close.

"I do." It was all I could say.

"That's right. You remember those words for later." He lowered his head, and his lips met mine in the softest kiss ever. "We were meant for each other, Sarah. We will figure out the best way to be together."

The conviction in his voice convinced me.

We would be together.

A look at Book Three: Sniffing Out Scandal

They say that a watched pot never boils...

Christmas is fast approaching, and Sarah Murray is overseeing Bishop's holiday fair operations while also preparing to leave her family-owned bakery to resume her career as a court reporter. And although she will miss the warmth that Layers Baker offers, she is dying to dive back into her true passion.

But difficulties arise when her long-distance relationship with Police Lieutenant Jake Charters is tested. Sarah's penchant for sleuthing and trying to solve town mysteries is something Jake wants her to cut back on, and—in true Sarah Murray fashion—complications go into overdrive after a friend asks her to investigate a missing eleven-year-old student.

When juggling a Christmas parade, a rocky relationship, and snooping prove to be too much—after finding out the missing girl's grandfather is a mule for a LA money-laundering operation—Sarah realizes she may have bitten off more than she can chew.

Ensuring this year's Christmas fair is the town's best one yet, Sarah must follow clues she cannot ignore… to once again sniff out a deliciously eerie scandal.

AVAILABLE JANUARY 2023